INTRIGUED BY LOVE

WRITTEN IN THE STARS - BOOK 5

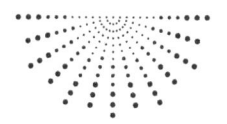

SIENNA SNOW

Copyright Page

Copyright © 2020 by Sienna Snow

Published by Sienna Snow

All rights reserved.

The scanning, uploading, and distribution of this book without permission is a theft of the author's intellectual property. If you would like to share this book with another person, please purchase an additional copy for each person you share it with. If you are reading this book and did not purchase it, or it was not purchased for your use only, then you should return it to the seller and purchase your own copy. If you would like permission to use material from the book (other than for review purposes), please contact authorsiennasnow@gmail.com. Thank you for your support of the author's rights.

This book is a work of fiction. Names, characters, places, and incidents are the product of the author's imagination or are used fictitiously. Any resemblance to actual events, locales, or persons, living or dead, is coincidental.

Cover Design: Steamy Designs

Editor: Jennifer Haymore

www.siennasnow.com

ISBN - eBook - 978-1-948756-16-7

ISBN - Print - 978-1-948756-17-4

WRITTEN IN THE STARS – BOOK 5

INTRIGUED
by Love

By Sienna Snow

FOREWORD

Dear Readers,

Do you believe in destiny? Or do you believe you drive your own fate when it comes to matters of the heart?

The idea for the Written in the Stars series came about one afternoon as I was thinking about how intertwined we are with the universe and the cosmos—we're made of stardust, after all. It got me thinking about astrology, and whether something as celestial as our Zodiac signs influenced how we behave in love. Some may call it pseudoscience, while others use their horoscopes daily to make major life, love, and career decisions.
That's how this series was born!

Twelve months. Twelve wickedly talented romance

FOREWORD

authors. All coming together to answer the age-old question—Does your horoscope decide your fate in love?

You'll have to decide for yourself as you binge-read your way through twelve deliciously sexy and deeply romantic stand-alone novellas—one for each Zodiac sign. I can't wait to start this journey with you. Personally? I think it was written in the stars!

XO,
C.M. Albert

P.S. Please join us in our fun and interactive Written in the Stars readers' group at https://www.facebook.com/groups/writteninthestarsbooks where we discuss all things horoscope and love related!

CHAPTER ONE

Kailani

"Want to hear your horoscope for the day?"

Raquel, my assistant manager, rushed through the open door of my office, holding a folder in one hand and her smartphone in the other.

"Not really," I said, looking up from a stack of papers detailing the events planned for the upcoming month at Lykaios Bora Bora, the luxury resort where I was the general manager and a shareholder.

"Oh come on, Kailani. Humor me, for once."

Raquel had an obsession with zodiac signs, numerology, and anything to do with predictions of the future. Most of the time, I half listened to her rattling on about what the sun, moon, and stars had in store for my future, but today wasn't the day.

By midday, the property was going to be swarmed, and it wasn't going to ease until the first week of the next month. My baby sister, Kalina, Lina Xander under her supermodel-movie-star persona, was marrying A-list Hollywood producer/director, Thaddeus Oliver.

Thad had decided a destination wedding was the least he could do for my sister and therefore decided to rent the entire resort for over a month. This also meant I had to do everything in my power to make sure my baby sister's dream wedding became a reality.

Though I never thought I'd be trying to orchestrate a traditional Hawaiian wedding in French Polynesia. Yes, the two cultures had similarities, but there were many stark differences, mainly ceremonies and traditions passed down over centuries. My mother's family could trace their Hawaiian roots for generations, and the customs were to be respected, no matter if any of my three siblings or I were in Europe or in the middle of the Pacific Ocean.

Good thing I had my mother and aunts and their almost daily check-in calls to help make it "just the way it's supposed to be."

"Pretty please." Raquel gave me puppy-dog eyes.

"Unless you can predict that this celebrity-filled, month-long wedding extravaganza is going to go off without a hitch, I don't want to hear it."

"We're in the hospitality industry—nothing ever goes off without a hitch. We deal with mercurial guests every day. What works for them in the morning could be a catastrophic disaster by lunchtime."

I couldn't argue with her assessment. The LB, as we called the resort, had a reputation for making everything perfect for its guests, which also meant dealing with moody clientele.

"Speaking of, did you explain to Mrs. Baker that it wasn't possible to extend her stay?"

Raquel sighed dramatically. "I did. Saying she was upset was an understatement, and reminding her that she signed an agreement stating she understood the limited time for her reservation made no difference. She had an epic meltdown, worthy of your sister's Oscar-nominated performance. But after I offered her a free four-night stay in the villas the next time she was in the area, she mellowed out."

Daphne Baker was a country music diva who came with an entourage of twenty and spent more time on vacation than on her music. In the two years since the resort opened, she'd visited the island four times. I knew as soon as I saw her on the reservation list two months ago that we'd have trouble with her, and arranging to give her a free stay was worth the cost of her leaving the island without an international incident.

"So that means we'll have an empty property for an hour or two before bedlam ensues."

"Why are you so worried? It's your family who's coming. I've met them. They're very relaxed people."

"It's not my parents or sisters or my brother I'm worried about. Even Thad is someone I love seeing. It's everyone else. My extended family and all the A-listers who'll show up expecting to have everything handed to them."

Even though Thad had explicitly limited who his

wedding invitees could bring, going as far as having security and background checks done on them, I knew some would bring people who weren't approved. This would result in a lot of handholding and headaches.

"At least most of the non-family and friends won't arrive until the week of the wedding."

"True. I just want everything to be perfect for Lina."

"It will be." Raquel handed me the folder she was holding. "Here's the list of room, villa, and bungalow assignments."

I smiled. This was one less thing for me to oversee. "Thank you."

"So want to hear your horoscope now that I've added back a few hours to your life today?"

"You're like a dog with a bone." I shook my head and then nodded. "Go ahead."

She beamed at me, taking the seat across from my desk, and scrolled on her phone.

"Ready to listen? It looks very important."

"Yes, just tell me so I can get back to work."

Ignoring my annoyance, she started.

"Dear Gemini,

"A blast from the past will force you to confront your dual nature.

"Love is in the air, but only if you are open to it.

"Remember, your heart can't heal if you don't examine the wounds."

The second Raquel said "a blast from the past," a vision of gray eyes flashed in my head. Eyes that belonged to a man I'd done everything not to think of ever since Lina had called me about having her wedding on the island. Eyes of the man I couldn't seem to forget or get over.

An ache burned in my chest, opening a wound that never truly healed.

"Shit. Kailani, what did I say? You've gone pale. Are you okay?"

Raquel's concerned words snapped me out of my panic.

"Yes. Yes, I'm okay."

"Was it the horoscope?" She tapped her lips with a finger before her eyes grew big. "Is one of the wedding guests an ex?"

I rarely, if ever, discussed my personal life with anyone on the island. It was easier to pretend I was all business instead of a hopeless romantic who was nursing a broken heart.

"Don't you have a banquet to oversee?"

"I get the hint." Raquel moved to the door.

"I know you did. I'm going to take the first transport to the airport so I can meet my family. You know how they'll never let me hear the end of it if I'm even a few seconds late." I glanced at my watch and winced. "Shit, I'm in trouble. Their plane from Honolulu lands in less than an hour."

"Don't worry about anything. I'll hold down the fort. Take care of your family. You're technically a guest for the wedding too."

I rolled my eyes. "If only that were possible."

"I'm going to make it my mission for you to have fun,

even if it means that I have to call in backup. Meaning your mom and aunts."

Thinking of my mom and her sisters made me smile. They had this way of getting people to do what they wanted without anyone being the wiser. Just like how they'd inserted themselves into helping me with all the wedding details when I could have managed everything without them.

On their last visit, Raquel had been "officially" adopted into the family. Which meant if Raquel told them I was overworked, they would close ranks and keep me from doing any of my hotel duties.

"Warning heard. I'm still going to make sure this wedding happens without a hitch. However, I promise to enjoy time with everyone here."

"Maybe someone in the wedding party will tickle your fancy."

I pushed down the dread her words brought forth and said, "Nope. Not interested."

She shrugged. "It was worth a try."

CHAPTER TWO

KAILANI

I arrived at the Motu Mute Airport just in time for the private jet carrying my family to touch down.

I couldn't wait to see everyone. My last visit to Honolulu, where my parents lived, was in December during a three-day stretch between Christmas and New Year's. I missed my family. Missed my bossy sister Kiana telling me what to do. And it was even worse ever since my brother moved back to Oahu with my sister-in-law, Cora. Lina lived on the mainland but was the one I saw most often due to her jet-setting lifestyle and Hollywood paycheck.

I made my way to the outdoor waiting area. The wind picked up, cooling my heated skin. Inhaling deep, I let the light floral scent mixed with the salty ocean air engulf my senses. I loved living in French Polynesia and especially Bora Bora. Yes, it was a tourist destination, but it was no way near as overwhelming as Las Vegas or Honolulu, where I'd grown up.

I couldn't wait for my parents, Colonel Isaiah Alexander and Major Malia Alexander to enjoy the beachfront bungalow I'd reserved for them.

Papa had officially retired from the Air Force after serving thirty-five years, most of it at Hickam Air Force Base, and he deserved some well-earned rest and relaxation. Papa was so much fun when he wasn't worried about getting back to work or taking too much time off.

Maybe he could get Mama to join him in some unwinding for a bit before the wedding craziness started. Though I highly doubted it. Mama had retired five years ago but still worked as a nurse on a part-time basis. She was one of those women who couldn't sit still and would rather work in a busy hospital than stay home.

My sister Lina had inherited my mother's drive. She'd moved to Hollywood to work behind the scenes as a production assistant and ended up in front of the camera when a designer told her that her unique Hawaiian and Black heritage was the perfect look for a fashion campaign he was putting together. As if overnight, Lina became a household name, which eventually led to her getting a role in a film Thad was producing.

My other sister Kiana and sister-in-law, Cora, were successful in their own right. Kiana was an up-and-coming photographer, and Cora was a cardiac surgeon. She was also five months pregnant with a little girl. My brother, Kevin, had followed Papa into the military but instead of making the Air Force a long-term career, he'd gone into private security with a group of friends. His company was in charge of making sure no one without authorization stepped foot on Lykaios Bora Bora.

The sounds of airplane engines booming around me snapped me out of my thoughts. A few seconds later, Thad's jet with the *Oliver Studios* logo came into view.

It pulled to a stop and a set of rolling stairs moved in its direction. After a few minutes, the door opened and I saw Papa standing there.

I jumped up and down with excitement. I was a grown woman of twenty-nine, but seeing my dad always made me giddy. He was a hard military man to everyone but his family. With us he was mushy peas, as Mama liked to say.

His gaze landed on me, and a big smile broke out on his face. Taking the stairs down two at a time, he walked to me. I rushed toward him and jumped into his arms.

"Oh Papa, I missed you so much."

He squeezed me tight. "Baby girl, I'm so happy to see you."

The feel of his arms around me gave me the comfort I'd needed ever since Raquel had read my horoscope and the worry about the past had crept in.

Kissing my forehead, Papa set me down. "Go say hello to your mama or she'll get jealous that I'm getting all the love."

I slid out of his hold, gave him a peck on the cheek, and then moved toward Mama, my sisters, and Cora.

My heart was so happy to see all of them. And being in

the company of my family for a few minutes felt as if it hadn't been months since I'd seen them. Cora was finally showing and it made my heart squeeze a little, reminding me of all the plans I'd had and how they'd evaporated.

Once we were done with our squeals and hugs, I asked, "Where are Kevin and Thad?"

"The guys were finishing a game of *Halo*." Lina rolled her eyes. "You know how competitive they get."

"It was more that Jax was kicking their asses and they wanted rematches," Kiana said.

My stomach clenched as if I'd been punched in the gut. "Jax is here?"

"Duh. He's the best man." Kiana studied my face and then glared at Lina when she shoved her.

At that moment, said man emerged from the plane.

My heartbeat immediately jumped, and all the pain of the past few years reared its ugly head.

I swallowed the lump in my throat.

God, he was gorgeous. Dark black hair cut close on the sides and longer on top. A face sculpted by the gods and a body I knew was chiseled to perfection under the designer button-down shirt and pants. He had a golden tan that was shades darker than the one he'd sported when we lived together in Vegas.

He oozed power, affluence, and confidence. Those had been the things that had attracted me when he'd joined a weekly poker game I attended with some of my coworkers at the casino where I'd interned. And the tattoos that covered his arms and neck gave him a rebel vibe one wouldn't expect in a guy who spent his days wearing a suit and charming his elite clientele.

I'd known he was out of my league from the beginning and tried to resist the pull he'd had on me. It had taken two months for me to agree to go out with him. Our first date had been the exact opposite of what I'd expected. Instead of wining and dining me as I'd expect any high roller in Vegas to do, he'd taken me to a go-kart park to race cars and play video games. He'd heard me talk about the outings I'd had with Papa as a child and decided to recreate one of them.

I'd fallen for him that night.

His gray eyes landed on mine, and without thinking I stepped back, bumping into Cora.

She steadied me, whispering, "Are you okay? I told them we should've let you know he was coming with us, but Lina said you were over him and not to worry. When I tried to text you, they took my phone away."

I kept quiet and continued to watch him. There was heat in his gaze, reminding me of nights spent bound to our bed and lost in pleasure.

"Oh yeah, they're definitely over each other," Kiana muttered. "Not. Tell us again that you aren't still in love with him, Kailani."

"Dammit, Kiana, leave her alone. I can't wait until Ani gets here so she can kick your ass," Cora admonished, referring to my other sister-in-law, Ani, the Kiana-tamer.

Kiana cocked a hand on her hip. "My wife will take my

side. That's what you're supposed to do when you get married."

Cora set a hand on my shoulder. "Ignore the comedian over there, take a deep breath, and go say hello."

I followed Cora's instructions, pushed the shock of seeing Jax away, and walked toward him.

I offered him my hand. "Welcome to Bora Bora, Jax."

Good, my voice hadn't quivered.

"Kai." He slipped his palm over mine and pulled me gently toward him, in the way he'd done with me hundreds of times. But instead of kissing my lips, he kissed my cheek.

Goose bumps pricked down my spine, and I had to resist the instinct to nuzzle into him. My body ached for him.

This was going to be a very long four weeks.

He smelled so good, of bergamot and sandalwood. The scent of the cologne I'd given him.

"Did you miss me, Little Bird?" He pulled back without releasing my hand.

My stomach clenched, hearing him use the pet name he'd given me. The one I hadn't heard in years, and reminded me of the last time we'd made love.

I tried to tug free but his grip tightened.

"Jax. Let me go."

"Don't you think I deserve answers?"

"This isn't the time or place."

"I agree—that was two years ago in Vegas. Before I came home to an empty house and a broken heart."

Tears burned the backs of my eyes. It wasn't as simple as he made it sound.

"Don't I get a hello?" Thad came up behind Jax, smacking his back and breaking the standoff between Jax and me. "Step aside, old man. I need to hug my girl."

Jax narrowed his gaze, telling me we'd talk, and then released my hand, moving out of Thad's way.

Thad wrapped an arm around my shoulder, squeezing me and then guiding me toward the walkway into the airport terminal. "Good to see you again, Boss Lady."

"Same goes," I said, rolling my eyes and trying to act calm and unfazed by the man walking right behind us.

That's when I realized Kevin was nowhere in sight. "Where's Kevin?"

"Taking a work call. He'll be down in a few minutes. Come on, let's wait for him in the van. In the meantime, you can fill me in on all the ways you're going to boss us around so my future wife gets the wedding of her dreams."

CHAPTER THREE

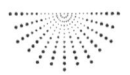

Jax

I stepped out onto the wraparound lanai of the Lykaios Bora Bora two days after arriving on the island and watched Kai on the beach below, directing her staff in something or another. She'd avoided me like the plague, finding something to keep her busy every time I was in the vicinity.

It had taken all my strength not to throw her petite body over my shoulder and find a spot to get the answers I'd waited over two years for. Trying to force her to do anything would have her shutting down, though. And I'd learned long ago, rushing her never worked. She would need to work through it in her head. In any other situation, watching her process, going back and forth in her mind on a problem until she came to a decision, would have been a turn-on. However, something told me I'd have to give her a nudge to get her alone or she'd stall any conversation until it was time for me to leave.

Kai gathered her hair, tying it back into a low ponytail, and caught me looking in her direction.

God, she was beautiful. Big brown eyes a man could stare into for hours, golden skin that she'd inherited from her parents that gave her a kissed-by-the-sun glow whether it was winter or summer. The woman could go barefaced, void of makeup, and still look as if she were ready to star in a movie in the same way Lina had charmed Hollywood. Then there was the body with curves a man could hold on to and was kept in shape from early-morning sessions of power yoga. She was so tiny, barely five-foot-two, but it never took away from the impact she had on people. She was a force that refused to let anyone push her around.

Even when she was in her bossy all-business persona, there was a sensuality about her that drew a man to want to break down her walls.

I'd thought I was that man.

I had no doubt her leaving me had been a spur-of-the-moment decision. She had this impulsive yet decisive nature that made it easy for her to jump feet first and follow through on a new plan.

What I had to find out was exactly the circumstance that had pushed her into moving thousands of miles away to the middle of the Pacific Ocean. One minute I was planning a future with the love of my life and the next, I was left to pick up the pieces of my soul that had been ripped to shreds.

She'd been my everything.

What the fuck had I done to destroy it? I'd all but turned my back on my family for how they'd treated her. She'd always been my priority. How many nights had I stayed up trying to keep the evil of my parents from her? Hell, I'd gone as far as telling my mother she couldn't step foot near Kai if she couldn't be civil.

One way or another, I would get my answers.

"Have you tried to talk to her?" Thad came up behind me.

Thad and I had been friends since we met as ten-year-olds during a summer basketball camp. We'd come from similar Hollywood backgrounds. His parents being the legendary Oliver Studios heads, Justine and Kristy Oliver. And my parents being multi-Oscar-winning movie royalty turned production financiers, Christopher and Jennine Burton. The one difference we had was that he adored his family and wanted to follow in his parents' footsteps. Whereas I wanted nothing to do with the exhaustion and drama that came with mine.

Thankfully the Olivers had adopted me into their fold, otherwise I'd have turned out like every other clichéd rich, over-pampered, and complete fuck-up Hollywood kid.

"It's kind of hard to when she runs away anytime I'm within a few feet of her."

"She still has feelings for you. It's obvious to everyone.

Plus, the fact she hasn't mentioned anything about what happened to her sisters says it all."

"How's that?"

"You know those three tell each other everything, not to mention adding Ani and Cora into the mix. Hell, I've heard enough conversations to know when all of them will start their monthly cycles."

The sad part was that I knew Thad was right. During the four years Kai and I had been together, I'd heard every detail about the women in her family's sex lives.

"Are you saying they have no idea why she left me?"

"That's exactly what I'm saying. You, my man, need to find out what the fuck happened before you make this move to the South Pacific permanent."

I winced and looked around, making sure no one had heard Thad's words. As far as anyone knew, I still lived in Las Vegas. Hell, I'd flown to Hawaii just so I could join the flight coming back to Bora Bora. Thad, as my best friend, was the only person aware of my living arrangement.

"Relax. It's just us here. By the way, you owe me. I keep no secrets from my girl, and this one is a doozy."

I felt a pang of jealousy. Thad and Lina actually had what I'd believed Kai and I once shared.

"How is my living arrangement important to your relationship with Lina?"

"Well, it does look a bit stalkerish to live on your megayacht offshore while you build a house on the very island your ex lives on, in hopes of getting her to fall back in love with you."

"Whatever. I can work remotely from anywhere around the world. I'm the lucky asshole who can afford his dreams of living in French Polynesia without being a bum."

That excuse seemed lame even to me. First, I'd have to figure out what the future held for Kai and me, and then I'd make the final decision on whether to reveal my residential situation.

"Keep telling yourself that."

I scrubbed a hand over my face. "I have to get her to forgive me. It's been torture spending two years without her in my life."

"So no beach beauties to help escape the lonely nights of being a reclusive billionaire?"

I glared at Thad. I knew he was kidding but even suggesting anyone to replace Kai made me want to punch him. I'd had the house built with Kai in mind. It had every minor detail she'd told me she wanted in a home. I'd burn the place down before I let anyone other than Kai live in it.

God, I was such a fucking wimp. Kai had no clue she had me by the balls.

"The only beauty I want is that bossy woman over there trying to give you and her sister the perfect wedding. I only wish I knew what I did so I could fix it. I'm open to any suggestions."

"You could always seduce her and then work backward."

"She isn't the casual-sex kind of woman. It took me over two months to go out with her in the first place. And another year after that to get her to even consider moving in with me."

"I want to ask you a question that I've held on to for a while now."

I glanced at Thad. It was rare for him to keep his thoughts from me. "Go ahead. I promise not to punch you."

"Were you really going to ask her to marry you the week she left?"

I closed my eyes for a brief moment, remembering my trip to my parents' house to get my grandmother's engagement ring and the over-the-top way I'd planned to propose.

"Yeah, I was." I gripped the back of my neck. "One minute I was getting approval to marry Kai from her father and the next, she'd moved to Tahiti without a backward glance."

"I know the answer already but it's better to ask and hear it from your lips."

I waited for Thad to continue.

"Are you still in love with her?"

I watched the breeze pick up and blow pieces of Kai's hair into the air.

"I never stopped."

"Then find out what you did to fuck it up and don't do it again. She isn't any happier than you are."

"That's the plan, man. But first I have to get her to spend even a second alone with me."

"I have faith in you." He smacked me on the back. "Plus,

you could always seduce her with that kinky shit the two of you were into and then go from there."

If only it was that easy.

CHAPTER FOUR

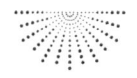

Kailani

I released a sigh, adjusting the cooling eye mask on my face as I enjoyed the aftercare following my deep-tissue massage. Lina, Kiana, Cora and I were two hours into our sisters-only spa morning.

The spa at the LB had a five-star rating and usually booked out months in advance. Luckily for us girls, Thad reserving the entire resort gave us unlimited access to services without anyone to interrupt us.

The four of us relaxed on loungers under an open-air gazebo, with a cooling water mister to keep us from overheating and an unending supply of fun beverages to provide hydration.

I couldn't remember the last time we'd had a chance to just veg together. I should have felt guilty for pushing some of my morning duties onto Raquel but I couldn't. Especially not with the way she'd gone to so much trouble to arrange this day with the girls.

I was seriously lucky to have Raquel in my life. Well, except for her need to tell me my daily horoscope. Today's said something about love waiting for me and not to let my fear rule my actions.

As if. It wasn't fear, it was self-preservation.

I'd loved so hard that it had destroyed me fraction by fraction until I realized how little I mattered. It was better to be alone than to be second to a family who'd never accept me.

Me having parents who weren't part of the Hollywood elite and who didn't come from money had always been a sticking point with Jax's parents. Well, more his mother than his father. From the first moment I met Tinsel Town diva Jennine Burton, I knew she hated me. She'd looked me up and down and treated me as if I were nothing more than the help. All she saw was that I was the daughter of a no-name Air Force colonel and a military nurse who worked for the people with real money. It hadn't mattered that I'd worked my ass off to be where I was.

In the beginning, Jax had run interference with her, but then he'd caved to the pressure and would literally disappear from our life in Las Vegas to handle something or another for his family. If it had been a one-off, I would have understood, but it turned into an every-few-weeks occurrence, and I was left to wonder if he was going to come back to me. It was as if I was a sectioned-off part of his life, one that didn't involve the part that took up most of his time or energy. He'd placed me in a tiny little compartment and would take me out when he had the time.

I'd dealt with it for far longer than I should have, and when I pushed back, he'd stared at me as if he had no idea what I was talking about. The last straw for our relationship had occurred during a particularly hard week where I was coordinating the opening of Lykaios Bora Bora while still living in Vegas. All I'd wanted was to spend a weekend in my apartment, with the man I loved. Jax had promised me time unplugged, just the two of us, no distractions, no anyone. When I'd entered our place, I found it empty. No note, no text.

He'd pulled the disappearing act again. I knew I couldn't live my life like that anymore. I wanted something permanent, with a future, a family, not a when-it-was-convenient-to-him relationship.

The next morning, Henna Lykaios, my direct boss and the head of Lykaios International had offered me the general manager position in Bora Bora. I was already a partner in the resort with a twenty percent stake. I'd invested when the project was a concept in Henna's eyes. It was every penny I'd saved from the time I started working at eighteen and the winnings I'd earned at the poker tables I played at in Vegas.

The investment had paid off in ways I hadn't imagined, thirty-fold, in fact, making me a very wealthy woman.

I'd decided it was fate telling me to cut my losses and start a new life. The move would bring me back to the island lifestyle I grew up in and felt at home with, and it would also put enough distance between Jax and me to keep constant thoughts of him at bay.

Now he was here. To remind me of all that I'd lost. All that I hoped for. All that I still wanted.

"Are you going to spend the rest of the month avoiding him?" Lina said, snapping me out of my brooding.

I lifted the mask and looked in her direction.

Damn, she was every ounce the goddess movie star. Even without a stitch of makeup on, her skin glowed. She'd say we all looked the same and she was partly right—there was no mistaking we were sisters—but I knew it was happiness that gave her the extra boost. Thad loved her in a way I'd only seen with my parents.

"I have no idea who you're talking about."

Lina rolled her eyes and glanced at Kiana. "Is she for real? She acts as if we don't have eyes."

"She thinks we don't know that her saying she and Jax fell out of love is bullshit." Kiana sat up and cocked a hand on her hip. "We deserve to know what really happened."

"Leave her be." Cora reached out and took my hand in hers. "We're here to relax. I don't want her to feel as if she's in an interrogation room."

I gave Cora an appreciative but weary smile. "This is why you're my favorite sister."

Cora was the only one in my family who knew the whole of what happened. She had this way about her that had people spilling their guts. A week after arriving at the LB, I'd called Cora to see how she was settling in to married life only to spend the next three hours crying my eyes out and letting Cora console me. She hadn't tried to solve my issues or tell me I shouldn't have run from Jax. All Cora had done was listen, and it had been the one thing I'd needed. I'd made her promise not to tell anyone the truth of why Jax and I broke up, and she'd kept her word, even with my brother Kevin.

In turn, I'd been the first person Cora told after Kevin that she was pregnant. She was as much my sister as the nutty two I grew up with.

"Fine," Kiana huffed and lay back down.

"Well, if Jax is off the list of discussion topics, at least tell us about the reclusive billionaire who built that mansion on the cliff over there."

I glanced in the direction of the gorgeous three-level building covered in balconies and windows. I'd watched it go up for the last two years. I'd wondered about the owner over and over. He was a mystery to the locals, always working with agents and intermediaries.

"I don't really know anything except he has a yacht he spends most of his time on. I've never seen him. The only thing I do know is that he designed the house for his lost lover. But you know how people like to romanticize things. I'm of the mindset, if he wants to be left alone, then leave him the fuck alone."

I rose from my seat and strolled to the edge of the gazebo giving the best view of the house in the distance. It almost looked like the sketch I'd made years ago on a napkin during a dinner with Jax. We'd talked about our ideal places to live and I'd come up with a house made of glass overlooking the deep blue waters of the Pacific Ocean. Back then, I'd always believed I'd return to Hawaii and Jax would be there with me.

"Maybe he's a heartbroken billionaire in need of company. The least you can do is stop by to say hello. Maybe bring him a cup of sugar. Especially since Jax isn't on your radar anymore." Kiana's voice was annoyingly sweet.

"Yes," Lina agreed. "It's the least you can do. Maybe he can help you get over Jax."

If only it were possible to get over Jackson Burton. Every time he was in the vicinity, my fingers itched to touch him, to stroke over his body, to relive the passion we'd once shared. Hell, he could be halfway across the world and I'd still want him.

I pressed the bridge of my nose and closed my eyes. I would not break down. This was for Lina, not about me and my fucked-up relationship with my ex.

"Girls," Cora warned. "This is supposed to be a fun day. I don't want her upset."

"Well then, maybe she can have a quick fling with Jax until we all leave," Kiana suggested. "I'm sure he'll tie you up and spank you for old times' sake."

I gave an exaggerated sigh, not turning to look at my annoying sister. "I have no idea what possessed me to share my sexual preferences with you two. It must have been temporary insanity."

"Well you actually live the lifestyle people write books

about. I'm fascinated. I'm not into it, but it doesn't make it any less interesting. Plus, who knows, I may get offered a part where knowledge on the subject might come in handy." Lina grinned.

I highly doubted Lina would ever accept a role with kink as a plot point. Her acting specialties lay within the vein of action or drama.

"It's not my lifestyle anymore." The thought of letting anyone other than Jax touch me with that level of trust or intimacy wasn't something I was ready to explore yet.

"It could be. Jax is here, and I'm sure he'd be more than happy to oblige your carnal needs."

"Kiana, you're like a dog with a bone. How the hell Ani puts up with you is beyond me. She probably broke down and married you so you would stop nagging her."

"But I nag so well," Kiana retorted. "If I recall, it was with your help that Ani arranged the proposal and elopement."

"After I couldn't convince her to drop your ass, I decided she was a keeper and the only way to make sure she never left was to get her to marry you." I shot Kiana a smirk over my shoulder. "Despite your laundry list of irritating habits."

I adored my sister-in-law Ani. She had a way of grounding Kiana and put up with her crazy ways. I really wished she could have been here for our spa day, but she was in the middle of finals for the classes she taught at the University of Hawaii and she couldn't leave until all exams were taken, graded, and reported.

"You think you're so funny." The pout on Kiana's face reminded me of when we were kids and I'd get on her nerves with something she had no comeback to.

"All right, children." Lina laughed and gestured toward a group of spa attendants who approached us. "It's time for our facials. You can fight afterward."

"I'm not giving up hope that you bang Jax while he's here."

I shoved my sister toward the doors leading into the spa. "Keep hoping. Sex with Jax is not an option."

Lina smirked and said, "Famous last words."

CHAPTER FIVE

Jax

A little before sunset, I sat down on a secluded spot on the beach to clear my head, to figure out a way to get Kai to talk to me and stop treating me like some random guest at her resort. I was on a fucking timeline and I couldn't lose this battle.

An hour earlier, I'd gotten word from my parents they'd be flying in a few days before the wedding and wanted to speak to me about my inheritance.

I'd ignored the message.

I neither wanted their money nor needed it. Besides, Hollywood wasn't where I saw my future. It was my parents' world, not mine.

I'd gone out on my own and with a few lucky breaks managed to build an investment portfolio that would rival the Lykaioses, who owned the resort we were at. Hell, my friendship with one of them, the middle brother Pierce

Lykaios, was what had given me the push to break free of my controlling father and mother. Pierce had a sordid family history that made it necessary to take risks and occasionally work with the unsavory element of life to succeed.

Taking his cues, I'd searched out any investment with high risk and even higher yield, mostly in international property development. Most of my business partners in the beginning were what one would call members of "organized families." They needed a way to enter legitimate business opportunities, and I provided the means to achieve this goal. After I'd amassed enough capital, I'd switched gears and moved into an industry that had been my love since childhood.

Yachting.

Well, more shipbuilding. From the time I was a kid, I would spend nearly every summer with my grandfather refurbishing old yachts that he'd bought for a bargain.

Pop, as I called him, had said manual labor helped him remember he'd come from a long line of men who worked with their hands. Pop had grown up working in the shipyards of Maine, helping with all aspects of ship building.

Pops would have probably remained in Maine, if he hadn't fallen for a Hollywood yacht owner's daughter who was vacationing there. Instead of my great-grandfather trying to keep my grandmother away from a lowly dock worker, he'd taken Pops under his wing and brought him to California and taught him the financing business of films.

Pops's love for the water had never waned in all the years he lived in California, and he'd moved back with Gran to Maine when he'd retired and passed the reins of Burton Productions to my father. Almost as soon as he settled, he hired a crew of five and started building small sailing vessels that he'd only sell if the mood struck him. I was lucky enough to inherit the last boat we worked on together before he passed away.

I'd started Burton Builders two years before I'd met Kai as a way to pay tribute to Pops and the home he and Gran had given me while my parents lived their movie-star lifestyles.

Today, the company was one of the premier custom yacht builders in the world. The ship I had docked off the coast of this island was the pinnacle example of the product.

"You're going to have to stop watching my sister like a man starved, or I'm going to have to punch you," Kevin said as he sat beside me on the sand.

"Fuck off, Alexander. I came here to be alone."

"It's just gross. The last thing a man wants to know is that one of his friends has seen and wants to see his sister in the biblical sense."

"You're such an asshole." I shook my head and grabbed the beer he handed me, taking a deep drink. "Besides, aren't you the one who's helping me build a house here for her to live in?"

Kevin had a lot of contacts, some of them in French Polynesia, who knew all the ins and outs of building in the area. Without him, I would never have gotten even the permission to buy the land, let alone permits to build. Kevin and I had grown close over the years and he'd actually been at my apartment the day I discovered Kai had left me with that stupid fucking note on the kitchen island. He'd flown to Vegas to help with the proposal I'd planned; instead, he'd helped me see past the end of the bottle and kept me from drowning my pain in liquor.

"Just for the record, she watches you too. Kai just doesn't make it as obvious as you do though."

I'd noticed the desire in her beautiful eyes over the last few days. She'd never been able to hide her attraction to me or how her body reacted to my presence. What pissed me off was her refusal to acknowledge there was still something between us.

I had to get the stubborn woman to speak to me, so we could get to the bottom of our issues and fix them.

I had a little over three weeks left, and I couldn't afford to lose another day.

"Any suggestions on getting her to want to be alone with me for even a second?"

"Honestly, no. I've never seen her avoid anyone. She's usually so in your face and straightforward that this is freaking my parents out too. Maybe it's time to ambush her."

"With your dad around? I don't think so. The man may be in his sixties but he isn't someone to mess with, especially when it comes to his oldest daughter."

I wasn't a weak man by any account, years of mixed

martial arts training and working on boats had kept me in shape. But I stood no chance against an angry father wanting to protect his baby.

"Then I suggest you sneak over to her bungalow and make her listen there. It's far enough away from the family that it will give you the privacy to get it out on the table."

"If this goes wrong, I'm totally going to blame you for suggesting it."

"Are you saying you're scared of a five-foot-two sea sprite with a temper?"

"That's exactly what I'm saying." I stood, handing Kevin my bottle.

"Where are you going?"

"To wait out Kai at her bungalow. Desperate times call for desperate measures."

∼

Kailani

"Is everything set for the trip to the motu?" I asked Raquel as I skimmed the last of the transportation schedule for the family arriving tomorrow.

It was near midnight and I was exhausted. Trying to balance time with my family and my duties as general manager were harder than I'd expected. No matter how efficient my staff was, the responsibility for the LB was on me. It was my job to check and double-check everything so the resort's five-star rating remained a permanent part of its future.

"Yes. One of Mr. Burton's vessels will arrive a little before seven in the morning and the staff will stock the ship and be ready for everyone for a prompt ten o'clock departure."

"Do you want me to stay behind to handle my crazy aunts when they arrive?"

Raquel folded her arms across her body and frowned. "I've got it, boss. Go play guide for your sisters and try to have some fun. Besides, according to your horoscope for the day, the next twenty-four hours will be one of your only chances to relax until mercury moves out of your sign."

"As if I needed an astrology prediction to give me that piece of news."

"Well then, what are you arguing with me about?" She lifted a brow with a smirk.

Raquel was right. The spa day had been four days ago and I knew this would be one of my few chances to relax under the Polynesian sun until high season ended in September, which was over four months from now. This trip would also give me a chance to check out one of Jax's new sailing yachts. I'd seen the renderings years ago, but it always was a thrill to see the actual product once it came out of production.

It had fascinated me how he'd run a ship-building company from landlocked Vegas, but then again, a private jet had allowed him to visit production sites whenever it was required.

We were lucky Jax had a client who lived in the Cook

Islands and had agreed to let us use her new ship for a few days.

"Before I leave, just another warning: my aunts and cousins are a bit over the top, but they're harmless. Don't let them steamroll you."

"Stop worrying. My family is no less crazy. I can handle whatever they throw my way."

I took a deep breath. "I trust you."

"Good, now go get some rest." She yawned. "I'm going to hit the sheets too."

After shutting down my laptop, I rose. "I'll see you tomorrow evening."

"Night-night. I'll lock up."

Fifteen minutes later, I parked the little golf cart I used to drive around the resort at the front door of my bungalow. It was a beautiful two-story home, with a private beach and views I could lose myself in for hours. I opened the door, dropped my keys on an entry table, and went straight to the wine fridge. After pouring myself a healthy glass of my favorite cabernet, I made my way up the stairs to my bedroom and changed out of my work uniform before walking onto the second-story deck overlooking the star-covered ocean.

Inhaling the warm night air, I took a deep gulp of my wine, letting the alcohol warm me, and stared at the gorgeous house lighting up the distant cove. It wasn't the first time I'd studied the beautiful home.

There were many nights I'd made up stories of the man who'd built the mansion, just as many of the locals would do. Sometimes even going as far as to think Jax lived up there and built the place for me. It was worse now because Jax was here, reminding me of the past, of what we'd shared. I knew it was childish to avoid him or pretend he wasn't there when every nerve in my body was very much aware of his presence.

Especially my libido.

I desperately wanted to feel Jax's hands on my body, demanding my pleasure, forcing me to accept my desires. It had been so easy with him. Hell, until he entered my life, I hadn't put a name to the things I'd always craved with a man. I needed someone I felt safe enough with to let them control my body, someone who wouldn't abuse the trust, who understood my need to let go. Jax had been the one to show me there was freedom in giving up control.

My sisters loved to tease me about the kink aspect of the relationship Jax and I'd shared but it wasn't something we labeled. It was a natural aspect of who we were.

I doubted there was ever going to be another man who could make my pulse jump with one heated look or have my core clench with an innocent touch on my back.

Setting my wine glass down, I rested my hands on the railing and closed my eyes. I could survive three more weeks. I had the willpower to do it.

"I'd give up a fortune to know what you're thinking about at this moment, Little Bird."

CHAPTER SIX

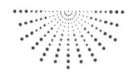

Kailani

My pulse jumped as I whirled around to face Jax. He leaned against the railing closest to the stairs leading down to the lower patio.

It was as if my thoughts, my memories had conjured him, but I knew the truth. It was his need to talk to me, to throw me off-kilter, to make me lose the control I liked in my life.

The energy burned between us like a livewire, just as it had been since he'd stepped foot on my resort. However, here we were alone. There was no escaping him now.

He looked so good. The rolled-up sleeves and open collar of his shirt gave a hint of the tattoos that covered his arms and body and made a woman glimpse the rebel under the polished businessman. The fact I knew every inch of him, the way he kissed, the way he possessed a woman, the way he fucked added to the anxiety now coursing through me.

"Why are you on my balcony, Jax?"

His slight smile touched his full lips, and he moved closer to where I stood. "You tell me what you were thinking about and I'll answer your question."

I retreated until my back hit the pillar near the balcony rail, realizing too late that I'd just put myself in a more compromising position than if I'd stayed still and stood my ground.

"Jax. This area is off-limits to guests."

What was the point of having a lone villa away from the resort if no one respected my privacy?

"Am I only a guest to you, Kai? The last time we were alone, I thought I was the man you loved."

Closing my eyes, I tried to hide the pain his words brought forth as well as the tears that burned my eyes.

Jax cupped my jaw, causing a startled gasp to escape my lips.

I stared into his stormy gray eyes, seeing the intensity I'd imagined so many times over the last few years.

He thumbed the wetness dampening my cheeks. "You wouldn't cry if you didn't still feel something for me."

"Feeling something for you was never the problem. It's how you felt about me."

Confusion flashed over his face, then hurt before it disappeared and was replaced with his standard cool mask.

"You were my world. My future. My everything."

I swallowed, not wanting to scream and tell him to fuck

off. If it was true then why had he let me believe I hadn't mattered, that his career, his ambition, his family were more important than me?

Instead of voicing my questions, I set a hand on his chest and pushed, but the man wouldn't budge. Instead, he grabbed hold of my wrists and pinned them above my head.

A shiver shot down my spine and straight to my clit.

He loomed over me. The heat of his body, so close to mine, added fuel to the fire of need he seemed to bring forth without trying.

"You don't believe me?"

"It doesn't matter. It was over two years ago." I made my best attempt to sound disinterested, knowing good and well I was failing. "We both moved on."

His hold only tightened for a fraction of a second before loosening.

"Is that right?" Holding my gaze, he asked, "How would you know if I moved on or not? You left without looking back."

I couldn't tell him that I kept tabs on him. To see if he was seeing someone else or if he found someone who fit into the world he was born into.

"Leaving was the only choice I had."

"Did you ever think that I deserved to know the reason you walked out the door?"

"It doesn't matter. It's in the past."

"Past? I think not." He leaned in, grazing his jaw along the column of my neck and causing goose bumps to pebble my skin. "I know every nuance of your body, and the way you're reacting to me right now says there is no past to us."

I bit the inside of my mouth in hopes the pain would help me focus and find a way to get him out of my villa, instead of how incredible he smelled, with hints of the sea, sunshine, and cedarwood.

"It's physical. You're an attractive man."

"So, any man would do to scratch an itch?" His erection pressed along the V of my thighs. "Tell me, how many men have stroked your body, tasted your skin, or lost themselves between your legs?"

His nearness was frazzling my circuits.

"It's none of your business."

"Did they know how you like the sting of a bite to your shoulder?" I couldn't help but moan when he nipped the juncture between my neck and shoulder.

My pussy flooded with desire, soaking my underwear.

He shifted my hands from above my head and wrapped my palms around the iron railing on either side of the pillar behind my back. "Do they know how wet you get knowing your man is going to make you lose complete control by forcing you to restrain yourself?"

My fingers flexed around the metal as my pulse jumped into hyperdrive. I shouldn't be doing this. I shouldn't let him make me remember.

It had been so long since I'd felt this type of apprehension and desire.

He shifted his hands to just under the swell of my bare T-shirt-covered breasts, causing them to swell and my nipples to pucker tight. Then he slid lower, down the sides of my abdomen, over my hips, and around the curve of my ass. "Did your other men know the kind of sexual experiences you crave?"

He lowered to his knees, and while holding my gaze, he traced a line from my ankles to under my skirt, until he reached my thong. Gripping the sides, he snapped the material with his fingers and let it fall to the floor.

"This isn't a good idea." My protest sounded halfhearted even to me.

He lifted a brow. "Then I guess you better say two specific words."

Little Bird.

His pet name for me had been a term of endearment when he'd used it, and I'd chosen it as my safeword when we'd started exploring the harder edge of the pain I liked to skate.

"Jax, please. This is only going to complicate things."

His breath gusted over my skirt-covered pussy, and I had to resist the urge to rub my pelvis against his mouth.

"That's the point. I want it so complicated that all you can think about is me." He lifted the material of my skirt and ducked underneath, making me shiver as his nose nudged the damp lips of my sex. "So complicated that you can't stand the idea of us being apart."

I clenched the railing, wanting so desperately to feel that wicked mouth on me. Two years without his touch, without his demands, without his seduction.

My battery-operated boyfriend was no substitute for

the way Jax knew precisely how to make my body sing. Hell, no man before him had known everything I needed, everything I wanted or dared to want.

He took a quick swipe with his tongue, grazing my clit and making me release the railing to grip his head. In response, Jax bit my labia. Not hard enough to hurt but to give me the warning sting telling me to put my hands back.

"Dammit."

"The rules are the rules. You want my mouth on your cunt, then you keep your hands where I put them. Two years apart couldn't have caused you to forget the way it was with us."

Why couldn't he let this be something simple, without a touch of the memories of our past?

It would be so much easier if this were just a quick fuck for old times' sake.

"Want me to stop?"

I shook my head. "No, please. It's been so long."

"Then keep your hands on the railing unless I give you permission to move."

Jax cupped my ass, drawing me closer to his mouth.

Logic said I shouldn't do this. That it was only going to cause me problems. But Jax had been the only man to touch me during the last seven years, and I needed to feel his hands so desperately, I knew I'd regret turning him down. I could give myself this one last time to indulge in Jax and then learn to live a life without him.

"Are the rules clear?" He spoke against my sensitive

clitoral nub and then followed it by blowing out a teasing breath.

My hands slid back into place and I folded my fingers around the railing. "Y-yes."

The pulsing in my core intensified to a level I hadn't experienced in so long.

The tip of his tongue grazed the wet folds of my sex. "Fuck. You taste incredible. I have to have more."

The next second, he pushed his shoulders between my thighs and descended on my pussy. Licking, sucking, devouring.

It was too much, too much. I screamed as an unexpected orgasm rocked through me. I gasped in air while holding the iron under my palms in a death grip.

"That's it, love. Let me hear your pleasure."

He held me against his mouth, working every ounce of pleasure possible from me. Then he wiped his soaked face along my inner thigh. He shifted from under my skirt, grasping the waistband, and tugged until the soft fabric pooled at my feet.

His gray eyes blazed almost black with desire as he took in my half-naked body.

God, what was I doing?

He rose, grabbed the hem of my shirt, pulled it over my head, and then clasped my waist in a familiar, possessive hold. "Yes or no?"

Why was he asking now? I was butt naked. Plus, he'd made me come harder than I'd come in years.

"Kai." There was a rumble of impatience in his tone.

"The only way I'm going to fuck you is if you say it loud and clear. I won't let you claim it was a mistake or some bullshit after. I know you better than anyone."

I wanted to argue but I couldn't. He did know me—my moods and my indecisiveness when it came to what I wanted and what I should have.

I gazed into his eyes, body aching for him, knowing nothing could come of this.

"I want you to fuck me."

"Thank God." He lifted me into his arms as if I weighed nothing and carried me inside. "I wasn't sure of my sanity if I had to leave here without burying myself deep in your cunt."

I pressed my face against his chest. I was actually doing this. I was going to sleep with Jax, consequences be damned.

Jax entered my bedroom and laid me on my giant bed, staring down at me. "Of course you'd have a bed as big as the width of the room."

I liked my space and loved the ability to roll around without worrying about falling off the other end.

"I'm still the girl I was in Vegas."

A shadow entered his eyes. "If that were true, you wouldn't be holding back. The woman I knew would have punched me in the face instead of running away."

I covered his lips. "Not now, Jax. I need to feel you. I've missed you."

As if my words eased the turmoil in him, he came over me, caging my body with his. He watched me as I worked the buttons of his shirt open and pushed it from his shoulders. He shrugged out of the cotton, throwing it on the floor, and returned with an arm on either side of my head.

I traced the ink on his chest and shoulders as I'd wanted to for two years. The patterns were a hodgepodge of sketches and symbols. Gliding my fingers down his chest, I found an area on his heart that had been bare the last time I saw him shirtless.

My throat burned as I read the words.

Aloha Aku No, Aloha Mai No

I'd translated those words' meaning "I give my love to you, you give your love to me" to him countless times while we were together.

"Jax." I couldn't hide the emotion in my voice.

He cupped my face. "Not now. Later."

He took my mouth, wiping out any and every thought but the way it felt to be in his arms. We kissed and explored, knowing exactly what the other enjoyed, exactly what the other needed.

When neither of us could wait any longer, Jax stepped from the bed to finish undressing and then climbed between my spread legs. His cock was thick, long, and hard, making my mouth water. He fisted it, pumping up and down, before sliding a condom on and positioning the head of his cock at the lips of my pussy.

He held my gaze and waited. For what, I hadn't a clue.

"Jax, now."

"Tell me, Kai. How many men am I going to have to erase from your memory?"

I reached up, gripping his forearms. "You're asking me this now?"

"Yes. I want to know. I need to know."

There was a vulnerability on his face I hadn't expected, and I found myself answering, "None. I haven't been with anyone since you."

"Thank God." He plunged deep, causing both of us to groan in unison.

I arched up, meeting each thrust, clawing at his shoulders.

"What about you?" I wasn't sure I wanted to hear the response, but I needed to know. "How many of the women on your arm have you fucked like this?"

He stopped moving, gripped my jaw. "The last woman I fucked, as you put it, was you."

Relief washed over me, and I grasped the back of his head, pulling his lips to mine.

It wasn't supposed to be like this. It wasn't supposed to be this intense.

He pushed in and out of me, working his thick, hard cock through my folds.

"Oh fuck. Harder, Jax. Oh God. Please, Jax. Harder."

My orgasm was close. I could feel it. I needed it.

He stopped and stared down at me, grabbing my hands and pressing them to the bed.

"No. Not again. What are you doing?"

"Answer one more question and I'll let you come."

I tugged at my arms, but his hold on my wrists was too

tight. My pussy quivered, needing the small push to go over.

"Why did you leave me? What did I do?"

I clenched my jaw, refusing to say anything.

He rocked against my clit, causing my muscles to clench around his cock. "Answer, and I'll give you what you want."

I shifted my face to look away from Jax's stormy gray eyes, but he caught my jaw again and turned me back to him.

"You forgot me. I was the lowest priority on your list. You dropped everything for everyone but me, your parents especially. It didn't matter how they treated me. I was tired of waiting for you to see me. To put me first."

He shook his head, as if he couldn't believe I actually thought that of him.

Instead of saying something to me, he lowered, kissing me with both demand and possessiveness, in the way he'd done when we'd first fallen for each other.

His thrusts resumed plunging in and out, increasing in tempo as he continued to devour my mouth. My body responded with a rush of pleasure and need. Everything ached inside.

Jax released my hands and they went immediately to his ass, urging him to give me what I'd only dreamt about for the last two years.

It was more than the feel of Jax in me and on me. It was the emotions his touch brought forth. I loved him so much that it nearly destroyed me when I knew there was no hope for us. I couldn't let him pull me back into something I knew had no future. Deep down, I knew it was already too late.

"Oh God," I cried out as Jax pinched my nipple.

"Pay attention to what's happening here between us. Not to the voices in your head. We'll talk about everything later."

He set a hard pace, pummeling my pussy and driving me higher and higher.

"J-J-Jax."

"Give it to me, Little Bird. Come in the way I've only seen in my dreams for the last two years."

He rolled his hips again to grind against my clit, and my body immediately erupted. Arching up, I screamed Jax's name and clamped down on his cock. He continued to thrust through my clenching and contracting vaginal walls.

My mind clouded with a pleasure I'd craved but hadn't experienced in years.

I held in tears that I knew would burst free the moment I was alone. It was only ever like this with Jax. The intensity and the passion. It was too much. It was too consuming.

Jax's rhythm became erratic and he bit my shoulder as he came. The pleasure-pain of the sting pushed me back up into another orgasm.

Jax gripped the back of my neck. "You're mine, Kai. I'm never letting you run away again."

CHAPTER SEVEN

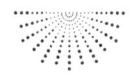

Jax

I'd barely shifted my weight from Kai and caught my breath when I felt her stir, pulling free from my hold and sitting up.

I grabbed her around the waist and pulled her back. "I don't think so. You aren't putting those walls up again. I meant what I said. I'm not letting you run away again."

"You don't know what you're talking about."

"What don't I know, Kai? From where I'm sitting, I lost the woman I loved because she thought I didn't prioritize her. When all I ever did was try to protect her."

"Are you fucking kidding me?" She struggled in my hold, and I let her go. "I was always left to figure out you'd disappeared to help your family or some project for your family. It showed me I was so important that I had to spend weeks at a time wondering if you were ever coming home."

I sat up. "Bullshit. I was working my ass off for your future."

"And you would run home to solve your parents' issues the minute they said jump." She stomped toward a chair where a robe lay.

Slipping it on, she tied the belt in a huff.

"You're angry about me seeing my parents?"

"No, I'm angry about you keeping me separate from your life involving them. You let them believe I wasn't important enough to include in the world you'd grown up in. Your mother told me this often enough."

"She did *what?*" I reached down, gathering my clothes before putting them on.

When the fuck had she been in Vegas? Fuck, it was probably during her monthly spa trips. I'd always assumed she went to Palm Springs, but now it was obvious—I was utterly wrong.

"Don't be so shocked. She showed up in the casino at the Ida Las Vegas at least once a month on her way to visit her personal spa consultant to tell me I was your side piece. That I'd never be the woman you would marry and not to get my hopes up. You were going to marry someone from your social circle. Four years I put up with it."

"I told her never to approach you. It was to protect you from her venom."

"Well, it didn't work out. And you running home to handle some crisis or another added fuel to the belief."

"Why didn't you talk to me? I would have cleared it up.

Dammit, Kailani, I wasn't ashamed of you, I was ashamed of them."

Her expressive eyes widened. "Then why did you drop everything whenever they needed you?"

"Because I didn't want their shit to pile up on our door. You were the one thing in my life that wasn't tainted by Hollywood or my family's elitist attitude or views."

Her shoulders sagged, and tears glistened in her dark eyes. "It doesn't matter, Jax."

"The hell it doesn't. You've convinced yourself I've done something I haven't. I want you to give us a chance to fix this. An honest chance. I want you, and I know you want me. The past wouldn't hurt you so much if what we had meant nothing to you."

"I won't make promises that I can't keep. Fixing things sounds so simple, but nothing has ever been simple between us."

"And what of love?"

"What about it?"

"Isn't the love we shared worth a second chance, worth fighting for?"

She closed her eyes for a brief second. A move she'd always done when she tried to ignore the truth of a situation.

"As I said before, love was never a problem. It was everything else."

She'd just all but admitted she still loved me. This woman was so frustrating.

I wanted to shake her. She'd shredded my heart, my

soul when she left. There was no fucking way I could walk away from her again.

I cupped the back of my head. "Name what constitutes everything else?"

"Your job for one, my job for another." She cocked a hand on her hip. "And the biggest thing of all, your family. They say jump, you say how high. It doesn't matter the cost to you and especially to me."

"Dammit, I explained I was protecting you from them. And you left me because of it."

"I left you because you assumed I would always be there and couldn't see what your disappearing acts were doing to me. You'd compartmentalized me and our relationship into a nice little box that was separate from every other aspect of your life. I was supposed to be your person, your woman. I would've stood by your side through everything, even your parents and their antics."

I took a step toward her, but she raised a hand to stop me. "I'm not finished. I left because I realized I deserved more, not just from you or your family, but from me. My love for you never changed, just what I would endure to keep it."

Tears streamed down her face, and she turned her back to me as she lifted her hand to wipe at her cheeks.

God. She truly believed I'd picked my family over her. How could she not see it was always her? What I did for my parents was to be free of them and make a path to her.

Had I fucked up that bad? Obviously, I had.

"Kai, I'm sorry. The last thing I ever wanted was for you to think you didn't matter."

She shook her head. "I can't do this with you, Jax. Let's leave it all in the past. I have a new life and a business to run. I have a wedding to orchestrate. I think it's better if we keep things professional from this point forward and chalk this up to unfinished attraction."

This was a hell of a lot more than something physical.

"Better for who?"

"For both of us. There's no point in rehashing things we can't change. It's not as if we have a future. I live in the middle of the Pacific Ocean and you in Vegas. Besides, long-distance relationships never work."

If she only knew what lengths I'd gone to in order to be near her. At this moment, though, she'd shut down and there was no convincing her how I felt about her.

I moved toward the stairs leading to the lower living area.

Just as I took the first step, I said, "Believe what you want, Kai. You're my future, always have been and always will be. I'm not giving up, even if you have."

CHAPTER EIGHT

KAILANI

"Want to tell me what the hell is going on between you and Jax?" Lina asked as she cornered me in the larger-than-average galley kitchen of the yacht we were using to cruise around Bora Bora for the day.

I'd avoided any conversations of significance with my family, Thad, and especially Jax. My heart hadn't gotten its footing from the moment Jax left my bungalow, and I'd let the tears and pain I'd held in for so long erupt. I couldn't make heads or tails of what Jax had said. We'd lived the same life and interpreted everything differently.

I'd spent the better part of the night and most of this morning lost in an endless loop of the same thoughts.

Had he really fought for me with his family? Was keeping me away from his Hollywood life Jax's way of protecting me from his mother? Had I made a mistake?

"There's nothing to tell. Jax and I talked, and we aren't

going to see things the same. I don't have time to sort through the mess of our past before he leaves again."

A frown marred Lina's perfect features. "Well, the least you could have done was end your self-imposed celibacy with the only man's cock you've seen in the last seven years."

"Are you for real right now? I tell you I had an argument with Jax, and you're telling me to sleep with him."

"Sleeping isn't what I had in mind."

My cheeks heated as the image of Jax fucking me flashed behind my eyes.

"Oh my God, you slept with him." She grabbed my forearm. "How could you not tell me? I bet you told Cora. You tell her everything."

If only Cora was down here, I'd probably do exactly that, but she was taking a nap on a sun lounger at the front of the ship.

"Tell you what?" Kiana asked as she came down the stairs from the deck above us into the galley area.

She studied me and sighed before walking up to me and wrapping me in her arms. "It's okay. He's not doing much better. Sex is supposed to relieve the tension, but it looks like the two of you just made it ten times worse."

I pulled back and muttered, "Thanks for the recap."

"You're welcome." Kiana wiped the tear I hadn't realized slipped down my cheek. "You love him, and it's obvious he still loves you."

I couldn't deny her assessment of the situation.

Lina set her head on my shoulder and hugged both Kiana and me. "Isn't there any way to fix this?"

"We have too much history to work through. Too many people and situations that have caused us pain." One of them being the woman who'd done everything to make my relationship with Jax harder.

Earlier in the morning, Raquel had received a list of expectations from Jennine Burton's house manager, Raymond. Among them being accommodations for her dedicated staff who would accompany her, so they could provide for her comfort when the resort fell short. It hadn't mattered that Thad had explicitly stated no one who wasn't approved was allowed to stay at the resort.

I'd personally called Raymond to convey that it wasn't possible to accommodate any staff or guests outside of those Thad had approved. It wasn't Raymond's fault his bosses were assholes, but I was not going to budge.

This resulted in an irate call from Jax's father, Christopher. I'd ended up giving him the same answers as I'd given Raymond, and told him if he still had issues to contact Thad personally.

Dealing with the Burtons had solidified that last night with Jax was a mistake. We came from two different worlds, and I couldn't see myself living in the one he'd come from, no matter how much I'd wanted to in the past.

"You mean Christopher and Jennine Burton," Lina said. "They had a conference call with Thad. Even got his parents dialed in."

"What did he tell them?" My stomach hurt to think Thad had caved and agreed to the demands of the Burtons.

"Give my man some credit. He informed them that due to security concerns, no one who wasn't on the original list and was cleared with a background check could attend. He went as far as saying he understood if they changed their minds about attending."

"I take it they didn't bite," Kiana said.

"Nope, but they aren't coming with an entourage of twenty." Lina threaded her fingers with mine. "See, Thad has your back. He's like the older brother you never knew you needed."

"I can't argue with that. I do adore the man."

"If you ever decide to separate, we're keeping him," Kiana added, and both Lina and I glared at her. Which caused her to burst out laughing. "You two were way too serious for a second. Almost reminded me of the sour look Jennine Burton had on her face that one time we all went to dinner in Vegas."

I shivered. "That was a disaster of epic proportions. Even my boss couldn't get her to chill out, and Henna has the ability to charm the grumpiest of guests."

"How a woman like her could convince the world she deserved an Oscar is beyond me." Lina sighed. "She puts a capital C in crazy."

"Well, I've already prepared my staff on how to handle her. I actually have Raquel assigned to be her guest services concierge. The less she sees me, the better it'll be for all of us."

Both of my sisters nodded their agreement.

"Now, back to the subject of Crazy Town's son. That's what Ani calls her, and I kind of like it." Kiana released me and folded her arms across her body. "Was it as good as you remembered it being?"

I groaned, knowing I shouldn't have expected either of my sisters to let it go. "Kiana, you're so nosy."

"Just because I'm not of the dickly persuasion doesn't mean I don't want to hear about your sex life or the man with the monster cock who rocks your world."

I should never have told my sister anything about my sex life or Jax's package. My only excuse was I'd been plied with tequila and we were on a sisters'-only weekend.

"I swear, Kiana. I can't wait until Ani gets here and keeps you in line." Lina laughed, then her expression grew serious as she turned her attention to me.

I braced myself. "Okay, let me have it. Unless I answer your questions, neither of you are going to let it go."

"I just have one and I'll leave you alone. Couldn't you just do something casual while he's here and then go your separate ways?" Lina asked.

"I don't do casual. You know this."

"Yeah, but it's Jax." Kiana braced a shoulder against Lina's. "Even if it isn't casual, you could pretend it is. At least you'll get a thorough vag servicing for the next three weeks."

"That's a great idea," Jax said from the stairs.

My face heated and I had visions of strangling Kiana.

How the hell had we not noticed him coming down?

How much had he heard? Well, I guessed I was about to find out.

Kiana broke the shocked silence. "Hey, Jax. We were just—"

"Could I have a moment alone with Kai?" Jax stared at me as he asked the question to my sisters.

"Sure. Come on, Lina. Let's go make sure Mama is applying her sunscreen and Cora is hydrating." Kiana grabbed Lina's hand and dragged her up the stairs without letting her respond.

Jax and I continued to stare at each other. Then, after a few seconds, Jax said, "Last night didn't end the way it was supposed to."

I leaned against the counter near the porthole looking out over the sea and gripped the edge. "I know. Do you think we can make it through the wedding without tension between us?"

He took a step toward me. "It all depends."

"On what?"

"On you." He moved to my side of the counter and continued to come closer. "On what you decide."

I frowned. "I'm not following."

"I want to see you, to be with you. At least until I leave the area."

I opened my mouth to argue, to tell him how it was a bad idea, that it would cause more problems and it wouldn't work, but he put a finger to my lips.

"Hear me out."

I sighed, ignoring the tingle I always felt the second he touched me. "Go on."

"There's no denying we still have feelings for each other."

I resisted the urge to roll my eyes. The tension between us was so high, my staff had started to make comments.

"You think there's no future for us."

"I know there isn't," I interjected.

He rubbed a thumb down my neck. "And no matter how much I disagree with your beliefs, I'll accept your stance. So, as an alternative, I have a proposition for you."

I lifted a brow and waited. I had a feeling I knew where this was going. And my traitorous body pulsed with anticipation.

"My proposition is exactly what Lina suggested. Until I permanently leave Bora Bora, we're together. We'll argue, we'll laugh, and most of all, we'll fuck like we're still the couple we were in Vegas. Whether it happens now or later, it's going to hurt when it ends." He paused. "But I'd rather spend my time here with you, not watching you from afar or having you avoid me."

I tried to digest his words. It was so much more complicated than the simple way he'd said it would be for us. I had believed I was going to marry him, have a family with him, live a long life with him.

Could I let it be a short fling knowing I still loved him?

But then again, could I give up the chance to be with him again, even if it was for a finite time?

"What do you say, Kai?" He set a hand on my waist, making my pulse jump.

When had he gotten so close?

I looked into his stormy gray eyes.

"Take the chance. You know you want to." His palm slid over my exposed abdomen.

Goose bumps prickled my skin and made me wish I'd put on something other than a crop top and shorts to cover my bikini. His touch was too distracting.

"I can't think when you're touching me like this," I said, unable to hide the desire tingeing my voice.

His lips quirked at the corners. "It's time to stop thinking so hard and enjoy the ride."

His fingers snuck their way past the waistband of my shorts and to the edge of my bikini bottoms. Immediately, my nipples beaded and a low throbbing pulsed deep in my core.

"Jax, my family is only a floor above." I arched into his touch, wanting him to go lower.

He flattened his palm, stopping the teasing movement. "Is that a yes?"

A moment of sanity broke thought the haze of lust.

"This is only going to lead to a broken heart."

"Can it get more broken than the way we feel right now?"

I had no argument against that. Could it hurt more than when I'd left Vegas? At least this time I'd know what to expect. Three weeks. I could do this. Then I'd go about my life here in Bora Bora and he'd go back to Vegas.

"Yes or no. The choice is yours." He moved closer, slipping his other hand to the back of my neck.

I closed my eyes, unable to handle the emotions in his gaze.

"Look at me." His voice changed to that deep timbre that affected me to the core of my bones, the one he'd use when we played our games. "I'm not going to let you hide. Give me your answer."

Lifting my lashes, I licked my lips, inhaled to steady my nerves, and then whispered, "Yes."

Relief flashed on his face before it was replaced by an intensity that matched the voice he'd just used.

I lifted my face, expecting him to kiss me, but he shook his head.

"You want me to kiss you, you'll have to earn it."

A tingle shot down my spine.

"You can't be serious. Here?"

He nodded. "You know the rules. Don't move your hands or come unless I give you permission."

"Yes, Jax." My fingers flexed on the granite I held on to.

He pushed his palm past the edge of my bikini bottom, through the soaked seam of my sex, and to my swollen clit. "Fuck, you're so wet."

His cock grew against me, thick and hard.

I bit my lip, trying to hold in the moan that wanted to escape. Dammit. I was loud when it came to sex, and I'd have to keep it in or my family would rush down here.

"Let me see if we can get you to scream."

I narrowed my gaze. "You wouldn't."

"Wouldn't I?" He circled the aching bundle of nerves. "Besides, I know you'll be a good girl and keep all those sexy sounds you like to make inside. I promise, I'll make it worth your while."

My pussy flooded with my desire as he drove up my need. I threw my head back and gazed up at the ceiling of the kitchen, trying to hold in the desperate urge to cry out.

Jax pushed two fingers deep in my pussy, and I couldn't help but gasp.

"Ssshh, baby. You don't want us to get caught with my fingers deep in your cunt. With your juices soaking my hand. With your pussy walls clamping down as I thrust into you."

"Jax, this is cruel." I inhaled deep and closed my eyes.

I loved it when he described everything he was doing to me. It had always turned me on when the refined businessman turned into the dirty-talking rebel.

He pulled out and then plunged in, repeating the slow motion, driving me crazy. "Tell me you don't like it when there's a chance of getting caught, and I'll call you a liar."

His thumb worked my clitoral nub as his fingers thrust in and out of my quivering pussy.

"Yes, but not the possibility of my parents seeing us."

"Then keep those moans internal."

Sweat sheened my skin, and my body was on fire. I could feel everything tighten inside. Just a little more and I'd go over. My damp palms slipped against the stone I held.

Jax used his other arm to brace me up, but I kept my hands where they were.

"Let go. I've got you. Come for me."

As if my body was waiting for him to give permission, the small spasms in my core turned into contractions, and my body detonated.

"Ja—" Jax covered my lips and drank in my cry of release.

He held me against him and kept me from collapsing on my unsteady legs. My pussy clenched around his pistoning fingers as wave after wave of ecstasy washed over me.

He kissed me, eating at my mouth, until the spasms stopped in my core and I slumped against him.

CHAPTER NINE

Jax

I held Kai against me, loving the sound of her shallow gasp and the feel of the tiny spasms of her cunt around my fingers. There truly was nothing on earth that could compare to Kai orgasming. Well, maybe coming around my cock versus my fingers.

I was hard as stone and could swear my dick had a permanent imprint of my zipper on it.

If only I could take her toward the passageway leading to the sleeping cabins and lose myself in her. But this wasn't about me. Kai's skittishness about me was something I'd have to navigate carefully. I wanted forever and had to do everything possible to make her want it to.

I knew it wasn't going to be as easy as seducing her. Getting into her bed was the easiest part of this whole plan. I had no doubt she still loved me, and after last night, I realized how deeply my family had interfered in my relationship with Kai. I was the idiot who thought separating her from the toxicity I'd grown up with and managed on a daily basis was the right thing to do, but I'd isolated her. And it had given fuel to my mother's need to control everything in my life.

I'd tried to do the perfect-son thing, letting my parents groom me to take over their company. Letting them go as far as choosing the right women to date. Not one of those women made me crave them to the depths Kai could with one smile.

I'd been a goner from the moment I took my spot at the weekly poker game Pierce Lykaios held with his brothers and I saw Kailani Alexander sitting at the table. She'd come from work and wore a custom-tailored designer outfit in fire-engine red. Her hair was pulled up in a knot atop her head. When I'd taken my seat across from her and she'd looked my way with a smile, it was as if my heart stopped. There was no doubt in my mind she was my future. It had taken time to convince her, but she'd eventually given me a chance and we'd been together ever since. Well, until that day I'd come home to an empty apartment.

Kai stirred as her breath leveled out.

"Wow," she whispered and pressed her cheek against my chest.

"I completely agree." I slid out of her wet heat and brought my fingers to my lips, sucking in her essence.

Her taste was better than any fine wine.

Kai shook her head at me without pulling out of my hold. "You're incorrigible."

"What? I'd lay you out on this counter and gorge on your pussy juices if I didn't fear for my life with your father and brother."

"Speaking of. We have to get upstairs or someone will come looking for us."

"We're not going anywhere until this matter is settled." I steadied her on her feet as she moved to stand on her own and then threaded my fingers through the soft hair at the nape of her neck. "I meant what I said. You're mine until I leave French Polynesia."

"It's only three weeks."

"Are you asking me to stay longer?"

She rolled her eyes. "You'd be bored out of your mind before you knew it. Life in Bora Bora runs on its own time."

"I can handle a change of pace."

She frowned. "Vegas is more your speed than here."

"Try me." I leaned in until our faces were a mere inch apart. "Give me a real chance and see what I'd do for you."

"Are you saying you'd move to Bora Bora for me?"

I held her midnight gaze and said, "Yes."

It wasn't time to tell her I'd already made the move. Hell, I'd built a fucking house for her.

"And run your empire from here?" She tried to slip away from me, but I trapped her against the granite.

I ignored the way my still-hard cock jumped at the slight brush of her body.

"Yes. There are these things called the Internet, satellites, and airplanes. If you recall, I worked from home most of the time when we lived together."

"You also have a business building ships. Don't you have to be at the ports?"

"I have staff that I trust to run production, and outside of any emergencies, I only visit sites quarterly."

"I don't want you to give me hope and then take it away. I'd rather go into this without expectations."

I clenched my jaw. "You'd rather pretend this a casual thing when we both know it'll always be anything but casual?"

"Yes. I can't let myself believe otherwise."

I wanted to be angry, but her vulnerability and honesty hit my heart like a fist. This was going to be a harder battle to win than I thought. No, that was a lie. I knew it was going to kick my ass.

"As I said, try me."

"What makes you think it'll work this time when it didn't before?"

"It would have worked if you hadn't run away and confronted me instead." Fuck, why had I said that?

"You're right."

Her response shocked the hell out of me. "You admit you shouldn't have left?"

"No." Her shoulders slumped. "I admit I shouldn't have left the way I did. It wasn't fair to you and to me."

So she believed leaving me was the right thing. My gut always clenched every time I remembered the moment I realized Kai was gone.

"I won't argue with you."

"Jax, are you sure this is worth it? I'm not going back to the States, especially not now. And if I ever do, it'll be Hawaii."

"Don't you think you're worth it for me to try?"

She closed her eyes and then opened them, indecision, worry, and hope all warring in her irises.

"I'll give you three weeks, as you proposed in the beginning and then we'll discuss it after the wedding. I'm not ready to make any long-term plans."

I wasn't going to get any more out of her, so I nodded. "Fair enough."

She licked her lips and glanced at mine.

There goes my cock again.

"Kiss me. We have to seal the deal."

Setting a hand on her waist and one behind her neck, I drew her to me. Her fingers slid into my hair. Our mouths met. Initially it was soft, feathered kisses, then we let it go more in-depth.

Just as I was about to cup Kai's breast, a deep throat cleared behind us.

We jumped apart, both breathing hard, and stared at Isaiah Alexander. Instead of the scowl I'd expected at him walking in on me making out with his daughter, he smiled.

"It's about time you two fixed the mess you created."

I had no response to the statement.

"Stop staring at me as if you're both fish with your mouths open. Your mom wants some of the 'special punch' she likes so much." He air quoted. "Before we left, the chef said he stocked the fridge with it and everything for snacks and lunch. Grab the pitcher and let's go up. What's the point of having such beautiful weather if you're going to hide in here?"

Kai moved toward her father and opened the refrigerator behind him. Handing him the container, she began to gather cheese and fruit. "Subtle, Papa, very subtle."

"What?" He feigned innocence. "Oh, good idea, I'm sure Cora could use a bite to eat. That baby's not letting her rest." Isaiah turned his attention to me. "Son, you going to help us or do you need a few more minutes to take care of that situation?"

"Papa," Kai exclaimed. "Seriously, you're a menace. Mama always said Kiana gets it from you."

"You may want to see him in that particular state, but no one else does, especially not a girl's parents."

With years of handling Isaiah, this whole situation was more comical than mortifying. He'd walked in on all of his daughters at one point or another. At least we'd never been caught doing anything more than kissing. I couldn't say that was true of either of the other two sisters.

"I hear you," I said, adjusting my shirt to cover my erection.

"Papa, I'm going to tell Mama what you did."

"What? She'd agree with me."

"Keep thinking that. Mama is as nosy as Lina and Kiana are."

I ignored the continued banter between father and daughter and opened the pantry cabinets, pulling out a tray before loading it with the snacks Kai had set on the counter.

A few minutes later, we took the steps up to the main deck. There was truly nothing like the views around the islands of French Polynesia. The deep blue waters with their array of wildlife gave an almost ethereal feel to the area. As did the untamed scent in the air that soothed the spirit, a mix of the volcanic soil and the bright foliage that covered the islands.

I truly never appreciated the stories of what Kai had grown up with until I'd moved to the area.

"Where should I put this?" I asked.

The Alexanders lounged on the deck as if the opulence of the yacht was no big deal. Kai's family had this way of enjoying any place they visited, no matter if they were having dinner in a tiny shack or spending the day on a hundred-million-dollar yacht, like today.

They weren't a family opposed to money, but it didn't define them. They believed only things one earned were worth having.

A complete opposite mindset to the one I'd grown up in.

Thad caught my gaze as he cradled Lina's head on his lap and gave me a knowing smile.

"Here should be fine." Kai pointed to a central table within reach of most everyone.

After setting the tray down, I took a seat near one side of the ship, across from Lina and Thad. Thad gestured with his chin in Kai's direction, then raised his brows in surprise when she came to sit next to me, lifting my arm around her and tucking herself against me.

I hadn't expected this, but I wasn't an idiot and would count this as a small victory in convincing her we had a future.

CHAPTER TEN

KAILANI

"Jax. Are you ready? We're going to be late," I said as I entered my bungalow, glancing at my watch. "You need to be at the fitting in thirty minutes."

I'd spent the morning getting most of the wedding guests settled with a quick break for lunch at a hole-in-the-wall place I loved after picking up my sister-in-law, Ani, from the airport. Now it was my duty to make sure all the groomsmen had their last fittings for their suits. Once that final task was complete, everyone could have a free night to do as they pleased before the wedding festivities commenced.

"Where the hell is he?" I muttered to myself and took the stairs leading to the bedroom. Jax had all but moved into my place since that day two weeks ago on the yacht.

We'd fallen back into the natural ease of living together, something that should have scared me. But it was an unexpected comfort, something I needed in my life, something I'd never had with anyone else but Jax.

As I made my way onto the landing, I noticed him leaning against the railing on the far end of the balcony. A grimness was etched on his face that could only have been put there by the arrival of Christopher and Jennine Burton.

Thad had volunteered to meet them and show them to their bungalow, and I'd jumped at the chance to avoid them, but I knew Jax had probably accompanied Thad. I could only imagine how it went. Most likely an hour filled with complaints and demands.

"Hey." I moved in his direction. "Is everything okay?"

He turned to face me and then set his hands on my waist. "What's your safeword?"

Goose bumps prickled my skin, and a low throb started in my core.

"You have a fitting. We don't have time."

"Already handled. Now I asked you a question."

I stared into his stormy gray eyes, seeing the need there, reminding me so much of the times back in Vegas when he'd come home from his trips to Los Angeles. He'd tell me that my touch was the only thing to settle him when everything else went to hell.

"Little Bird." I licked my lips, holding his gaze.

"You will use it if it goes beyond what you can handle. I need to trust you, just as you have to trust me."

I understood why he was saying this to me. Long ago, when we'd first become a committed couple, I'd refused to say my safeword and wanted to go further, but he'd known

I'd reached my limit and stopped. It had been one of our first major arguments. After that day, I never allowed myself to push beyond my limit, and I honestly communicated how I was feeling during a scene.

"Yes, Jax. I promise to use it if it becomes too much."

As if accepting my words, he nodded and then released my waist and stepped back to lean against a pillar. "Strip."

"Here? Where any of my nosy family could see us if they came by?"

"No one will come. Everyone is too busy with plans for their free night."

"Oh." I'd forgotten.

His lips curved, softening the hard edge on his face from moments earlier when I'd found him. "Strip. I want to see that gorgeous body."

My fingers went to the buttons of my shirt, unfastening each one slowly—the exact way he liked for me to undress.

Heat grew in his eyes, making my pussy grow slick with desire.

"Keep going."

I shrugged out of my shirt, letting it fall to the floor. I opened my slacks, pushing the material down to pool at my feet.

Just as I was about to unclasp my bra, Jax said, "Fucking perfect."

The huskiness of his voice added to the arousal coursing in me. His hot gaze felt almost like a caress.

"Keep going, Little Bird. I have plans, and they require complete access to every part of you."

My heartbeat jumped. I knew that meant a mix of pleasure-filled pain and orgasms that might have me walking unsteadily tomorrow.

In the next minute, I stood before him naked, my underwear piled on top of my other clothes.

"Come here."

I moved in his direction, stopping when I was a foot from him.

He studied me, not touching me, but taking in every inch of my exposed skin.

"I've kept it pretty tame up until now. I want to take you to the edge we last visited in Vegas. Tell me now if it's something you don't want to do. Once we start, I won't stop unless I hear your safeword."

I'd wondered if we'd ever go past the bondage and mild pain. I knew he'd been holding back. Why he was doing that, I wasn't sure. But I was happy he'd worked through whatever it was that kept him from taking us to that place we both craved.

I set my hands on his chest, standing up on tiptoes. His palm cupped my ass, drawing me against him.

I tilted my head up to look in his eyes. "I want it. I won't change my mind."

"That doesn't mean you won't safeword if you need it." He threaded his fingers into my hair. "Do I make myself clear?"

"Yes, Jax. I will safeword if I can't take it."

"Good." He lowered his lips to mine, taking them in a soft, gentle kiss.

When he pulled back, his whole demeanor changed. He wasn't my Jax anymore, but my Dom. We'd never called anything we did by formal names, but it was a given what we were. Only during the times we'd visited formal clubs had we ever identified ourselves as submissive and Dominant.

"Ready?"

"Yes." My body was on full alert and ready for anything he planned.

"Close your eyes."

I followed his direction, and a few seconds later, a soft material settled over them before Jax tied it securely behind my head. All my senses fired with the loss of my eyesight. The birds and the ocean sounded louder, the scent of flowers and earth were more potent, and the feel of the breeze along my skin was like an intimate caress.

Then he took my hands, placing a small object in each one. "Do you know what these are?"

Immediately, the hairs on the back of my neck pricked as I realized what I held. I could see in my mind's eye the colorful nipple clamps made of platinum and adorned with rubies and sapphires. There was no doubt in my mind that they were the same ones we'd used countless times in Vegas.

I'd left them behind, along with every gift he'd given me, knowing seeing them would be too painful and remind me of all that I'd lost.

"Nipple clamps." My voice was hoarse. "Why would you

bring these here, when there was no guarantee we'd get back together?"

Shit, why'd I say that? We weren't permanently together. This was temporary.

"They are always with me wherever I go, as are other pieces I gifted you, as well as some I never got a chance to give you."

Hurt laced his words and made me regret asking the question. Right now wasn't the time for this discussion.

"Jax—"

He cut me off. "Lift your arms, but don't drop the clamps."

I desperately wanted to bring us back to where we were only a few moments ago.

He stepped closer, brushed his lips over my forehead, and took each of my hands, raising them above my head. Slowly, he wound a soft fabric around each of my wrists and then attached my bound hands to something above me. I could move, but there was only a limited amount of give.

How had I not noticed this setup on my balcony? Probably because I was too focused on the man who turned my insides into mush.

"Damn, I've dreamt about you like this for over two years." He cupped my breast and ran his thumb over the tight bud of my nipple. "Remember, you have to let me know if things become too much."

"I won't make the same mistake I made in the past."

As soon as the words were past my lips, I thought of

other mistakes I'd made, leaving as I had being one of them.

Jax tapped a finger to my knuckles, snapping me out of my thoughts. Instinctively, I opened my hands, letting him pluck the clamps from my palms.

He moved behind, fisting my hair and pulling my head back. "I want to hear every moan, every sigh, every cry. No holding back. Is that clear?"

I swallowed. "Yes, Jax."

"Good." His mouth brushed the skin along the column of my neck, and then he bit, not hard enough to break the skin but with the right amount of force to cause my pussy to flood with need and desire.

"More," I gasped. There truly was nothing like that tinge of pain to heighten my need.

He kissed the spot where he'd bitten. "In due time. At this moment, I want to decorate those beautiful breasts of yours."

He circled back around until he was in front of me. His intoxicating scent filled my nose. Jax gripped my waist, drawing me toward him and enclosing his lips around one straining bud. He sucked and teased until I thought I'd go out of my mind from the delicious torture. Before I knew what was happening, he replaced his mouth with his fingers, pinching my aching nipple and then attaching the jaws of the jeweled clamp.

"Fuck." I closed my eyes as a tear slid down my cheek from the pressure.

He tightened the clamp, skating the edge of my threshold point.

I panted out shallow breaths, feeling my head go light.

"Breathe slowly, baby. Let the endorphins work their magic."

Gradually the pain morphed into a dull ache, and I wanted more of the erotic sensation.

"Ready for the next one?"

"Yes, please, Jax." I let my head drop backward and allowed the pleasure-filled pain to engulf me.

Jax repeated the process on the other nipple.

"Oh God, it's been so long," I moaned. "I needed this so much."

"So have I. Your body was meant to be decorated with jewels. Fucking beautiful."

A warm breeze slid along my sensitized nipples, and I couldn't help but whimper.

"Want more?"

"Yes." I'd take anything else he had planned if it meant I'd stay in this blissful state.

A chair scraped along the floor of the balcony, stopping when it brushed my knees. Jax sat, grabbing the backs of my knees and spreading them to straddle his thighs. The fact he'd tied me with the right amount of rope where I wouldn't strain if he pulled me onto his lap, told me he'd planned this longer than I'd initially thought. He'd taken into account my height with his and that of the chair as he sat in it.

"How long have you been planning this scene?"

He glided his fingers along the sides of my body, moving from my thighs up to my waist until he reached my upper arms.

"That's need-to-know information. And you don't need to know."

I'd have laughed if I wasn't aroused more than I'd been in years.

His thumb grazed my engorged clit, making me jump. "Ready for me to clamp two last places before I fuck you senseless?"

His words had my desire and trepidation coursing in my gut. "Oh God, you brought those too."

A wicked chuckle erupted from his lips, just as he pressed them to the valley between my breasts, rubbing his day-old stubble against my skin. "The clamps were made as a set. It would only make sense to use them all."

"Are you sure? It's been a long time since I've gone that far."

"I wouldn't take you to that edge unless I knew you could handle it." He lifted his head and blew on one aching nipple, making me hiss. "But if you'd rather not, you can always say two specific words. We will stop, and I'll make love to you as we have over the last few weeks. Both ways end in orgasms for you."

As much as he was the one calling the shots, this was about me, my pleasure, my needs. No wonder I'd never gotten over him. It was beyond sex, but I couldn't focus on that right now, or I'd have to think of how I was going to manage after it ended.

Inhaling deep, I said, "I want it. Show me the delicious edge I've craved for so long."

"You're soaked." He traced the seam of my labia back and forth. "I can't wait to taste. But first, I have to adorn this sexy cunt."

He pushed a finger into my pussy, pumping in and out, rubbing the bundle of nerves deep inside, bringing me to the point of release before pulling out.

"Jax." My bound arms jolted.

He spread my lower lips apart, clamping first one side and then the other.

"Oh God. Oh God. Oh God." My mind and body whirled with pain-filled pleasure.

I screamed the second Jax's tongue swiped over my exposed clit, an overload of sensation coursing through every inch of me. I jerked and thrashed.

It was too much. It wasn't enough. I was losing my mind.

Jax feasted on my pussy as it responded to every stroke, thrust, and lick. My core contracted, first in small ripples and then hard waves until my orgasm washed over me.

I continued to ride out my release, barely registering when Jax released my bound arms and carried me inside to my bed.

After laying me on the comforter, he tugged off my blindfold. It took a few seconds for my eyes to adjust to the light, but once my vision cleared, I focused on Jax kneeling between my legs, naked and glorious.

His cock stood straight out and dripped with precum.

He leaned down, gently taking hold of the clamps on my labia, and released them. I arched up, feeling a wave of dizziness as sensation returned to the engorged tissue. Jax kissed the spots where the clamps had been and then moved up my torso until he reached my nipples.

He looked up at me. "Ready?"

I inhaled deep. People believed genital clamps caused more sensation than nipple clamps, but for me, it was the reverse. As much as I loved the wicked agony, a few times I'd nearly passed out from the onslaught of feeling.

"Yes." I cupped his face, asking without words for him to kiss me.

He complied, covering my mouth with his as his hands went to my nipples, releasing the clamps.

I gasped, breaking the kiss, and instead of getting a fuzzy head, an orgasm crashed through me. That was the only cue Jax needed to thrust his hard cock deep into my pussy.

My core rippled around his length as he rode me hard, keeping the tide of release going.

My nails dug into his shoulders, urging him to give me more. "Jax. Harder, please. I'm going to come again."

He pummeled my pussy, holding me on the cusp of going over, working his cock in and out of me.

Sweat beaded down the side of his face, and he held my gaze. "This is us, Kai. I'm never letting you forget it again."

Instead of responding to him, I clenched my eyes tight and came again—this time bringing him with me.

CHAPTER ELEVEN

Kailani

"Come on, Kai. If your mom is out here, you better join us," Papa's baby sister, my Aunt Summer, shouted from around the giant bonfire we'd set up on the beach. "It's not in my genetics to move my hips this way and I'm dancing."

Aunt Summer cocked her hips from side to side in an exaggerated fashion that gave me visions of her knocking people down with her voluminous butt. I knew she was doing it on purpose to make a point. From as far as I could remember she would join us whenever we danced the hula, and after all these years, she was ten times better than the average mainlander.

"It's your baby sister's bride night. Don't disappoint her," another of my aunts said.

Bride night was my family's version of a bridal shower. It was a celebration of the Hawaiian aspect of our culture.

The food, the music, and the dancing were rituals for a girl leaving her parents' home for a new one.

"Maybe she's tired of moving her hips, since she's been shaking them for that Jackson boy again." Aunt Summer gave me a wicked smile that said she'd want details later. "I heard you've been hot and heavy for weeks."

I felt the heat rise to my cheeks.

Jax and I were back where we were when we had first fallen in love. It was easy. We talked as if we'd never been apart and shared so much, even discussing our work. Outside of one brief conversation about his parents where he said they weren't a factor in our relationship because he had nothing to do with them, we hadn't touched on the subject.

It wasn't as simple as he made it out to be, but I accepted it for now. Besides, now that the evil king and queen were here, I'd see how things would really be between Jax and me with them around.

My cousins started *ooh*ing and then began asking questions about Jax's virility.

Nosy-assed women.

I swore, Papa's side of the family was utterly nuts and had no filter.

"Yes, Kailani. Tell us about Jax and his bedroom games, or show us how it's done. Wasn't it Shakira who said hips don't lie?" a cousin from Mama's side added.

Strike that, my whole family was nuts.

That was when my mom's younger sister, Auntie Kata, pulled out the big guns and said, "You need to make your

Tutu Nima proud by showing us that all of the hours she spent teaching you hula weren't for naught."

I glared at her. "Using Tutu Nima against me is punching below the belt."

She shrugged her shoulders. "I use any and all ammunition at my disposal."

When I was born, Tutu Nima had still been in relatively good health and as the eldest female on my mother's side, she'd taken it upon herself to pass on Hawaiian traditions that dated back for generations. This included the hula.

She'd had me in a *pā'ū*, a hula skirt, as soon as I could walk. She wanted me to learn the "real" hula as she called it before I learned the *hula 'auana*, the dance most of the world associated with hula.

"Come on, Kai. You know you're a kickass dancer. I'm the one who was dubbed hopeless by Tutu Nima." Kiana dramatically sighed. "Although it never got me out of lessons."

Ani nodded her agreement. "Yeah, she really sucks. Come on. Show us novices how it's done."

I narrowed my gaze at her. "I was really happy you finally arrived. Now, I'm having second thoughts. You're as big of a pain in my ass as Kiana."

"Of course, she is. That's why we're perfect for each other." Kiana beamed in my direction. "Are you going to woman up or not?"

Technically, I wasn't a guest, and it felt awkward to participate even though this was for my sister.

I looked around, and it felt like all the women on the

beach had grown quiet and watched me. Thank God none of the men were around for fear of death.

For the women of my family, the bride night was a sacred time to celebrate the passage of a female from girl to woman. It was sexist as hell, but getting married meant a girl was no longer a maiden. The only males allowed were toddlers or babies who needed to be with their mothers.

According to my aunts, the presence of men took away the intimacy of the evening and added an unnecessary stress, since men required "attention" or they'd pout. Therefore, my aunts had threatened anyone with a penis with severe bodily harm if they dared to trespass.

"Come on, baby girl. Do it for me." Mama touched my chin. "Do it for old times' sake."

Damn, this was peer pressure to the max. It wasn't as if I was embarrassed, but I was in work mode. Then again, this was my family, my friends, my staff.

"I'm not dressed for it." I tried one more time to let logic reign. "Linen pants aren't going to move the way we want. Besides, we have a group of experts waiting over there to perform and teach everyone."

I pointed to where the resort dancers stood.

Instead of helping my cause, they brought forward three *pā'ū* skirts.

One of them went as far as to shout, "Show us those moves your Tutu Nima taught you, boss. I'm sure we can learn something from you."

"Well, that settles it," Lina said as she grabbed our outfits and ran toward me. "No excuses. Let's go, big sis.

It's my wedding, after all. Besides, it's been forever since the three of us danced together."

She was right. The last time Lina, Kiana, and I danced was three years ago after Tutu Nima's funeral. It had been her wish for us to dance at the beach fire in her honor. It had been bittersweet. We'd laughed, cried, and remembered the amazing woman who'd been our grandmother.

"You planned this, didn't you?" I studied Lina.

She gave me the innocent face that she'd give me when she was five and taken something she wasn't supposed to. "I have no idea what you're talking about."

"You just happened to have a *pā'ū* skirt and top ready for all of us to change into?"

"Does it matter? Let's go put them on and have some fun. You've become a workaholic. It's time to cut loose."

I glanced at Cora for help, but she just waved me toward the dressing tents. "I'll join you at the end. This belly isn't ready for your level of hula unless we want to change this to a birthing party."

"I seriously get no respect," I muttered to myself. "It's not appropriate for me to wear a bikini top in front of the hotel guests."

"Thad rented the whole resort—the only people here are the staff and our friends and family. Stop stalling and get to it."

I sighed dramatically. "Fine. But you owe me."

"I promise to make it up to you."

Fifteen minutes later, Lina, Kiana, and I were in our matching bright-red bikini tops and long skirts.

"One thing is definitely true about the Alexander sisters. You are hot as fuck!" Ani exclaimed as we came into view. "Wouldn't you agree, Cora darling?"

"Absolutely. It makes sense why Kevin hated having his friends come over when they were kids. These women have curves for days."

I couldn't help but smile. Cora couldn't say a mean thing about anyone.

"You're really my favorite person on the island." I blew Cora a kiss.

"Of course, I am. Plus, I threatened Kevin with bodily harm if he brought any of the guys here so you should double love me."

"Absolutely." I took Lina's and Kiana's hands in mine and we walked toward the bonfire.

We were greeted with cheers and shouts from all our female family and friends. Everyone's enthusiasm had us laughing. These were my people. The ones who knew my roots, who knew all of my crazy and still loved me.

"Are you ready?" I asked as we got into position near the bonfire.

The girls nodded, and I gestured to the musicians to start.

The sound of the *pahu*, also known as the hula drum, echoed into the night, signaling the beginning of the dance. My mother moved forward and started the *oli*, a chant to accompany the hula we were about to perform. My sisters and I responded in unison to Mama's melodic voice. She spoke of a love story from the past, one filled with love, struggle, and triumph.

We went back and forth for a few minutes, and then when my aunties' voices joined Mama's, I knew it was time for the hula to start.

I closed my eyes as the drums grew louder, letting the rhythm flow into my mind. I lifted my arms and cocked my hip to the side, resulting in a roaring round of claps and continued cheers.

Yeah, I still had it.

The beat flowed into me, and as if we'd never been apart and practiced every day, Lina, Kiana, and I lost ourselves in the music of my mother's people.

CHAPTER TWELVE

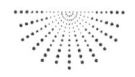

Jax

"If we get caught, I'm totally throwing you to the swarm of angry women who will beat you to death," I said to Thad as we took the long way toward the beach where the women were having their bride night. "Best friend or not, I am not taking one for the team."

"I'm the groom. They wouldn't touch me."

"I wouldn't be so sure about that," Kevin said. "I'm related to them by blood but I know my mother will pop me on the head with a mallet if she catches me crashing Lina's bride night. Not to mention my pregnant wife."

I couldn't see sweet, even-tempered Cora mad, even with Kevin.

"Then why are you here with us?" Thad lifted a brow.

"Because he's not going to miss the chance to see his woman dancing the hula in a barely-there outfit," I answered for him.

"As if you don't want to see my big sister in the very same outfit? Anyone around the two of you knows things aren't over. If I didn't want you two together, I'd punch you in the face for the way you watch her."

"I've never hidden I wanted her back."

"Then I guess you better figure out why she left you in the first place."

I had the answer but I wasn't going to share that information with them. I had to convince Kai she was always a priority, never second to anyone.

"Believe me. I'm working on it."

"I take it she's giving you a hard time." Kevin smirked.

He knew Kai was the most stubborn of all the Alexander women. Once she made a decision, that was it.

I grunted. "That's an understatement. She'd rather be my fuck buddy than my wife."

Thad ducked under some trees as we made our way closer to the beach. "I assume that means you and Kailani are fucking again."

"I really don't need to hear that shit." Kevin covered his ears. "She's my sister, man."

"And you knocked up Cora by spontaneous combustion?" Thad countered.

"I wouldn't say spontaneous, but there was combustion."

"Asshole."

"Hey, you started it."

Instead of letting them go on with the back-and-forth, I said, "I neither confirmed nor denied Thad's statement."

"You're both jackasses. Come on." Kevin pushed past us. "Follow me. I know a shortcut. I discovered it a few months back when Cora and I surprised Kai with a visit."

The music grew louder as we neared and then I stopped in my tracks as I saw the women dancing on the beach.

Fucking hell, Kai was gorgeous. The light of the fire added a bright gold glow to her beautiful skin. And the way she moved her hips had my cock jumping to attention.

The last time I'd seen her do the hula was when we lived together in Vegas and she'd gone down to oversee one of the shows debuting at the property she managed. There was a Hawaiian theme to one of the numbers, and Kai was not going to let anyone do a half-assed job on anything that represented her culture.

She'd marched onto the stage and showed the dancers how things were done. I'd been so turned on by the time lessons had finished that we'd fucked like rabbits for nearly the whole night.

As if sensing me, Kai's gaze shifted to land on me. She made no outward sign of letting anyone know we were there. Instead, she continued the motion of her hips and arms, dancing, turning, and swaying.

Then all of a sudden, the tempo changed and the music went from a traditional cadence to something modern. It was a mix of dance, hip-hop, and classical hula beats. The women who were watching rushed toward the girls and they all danced together.

However, I knew Kai's attention was on me. She kept the gyration of her hips going throughout the various changes in tempo. Her skill and confidence reminded me of the way she knew just how to drive me nuts as she rode my cock hard and without restraint.

Kai was a temptress, put on earth to drive me nuts. Without thinking, I walked toward the beach. I had to touch her.

"Where the fuck are you going?" Kevin called after me.

"Asshole," Thad shouted. "They're going to kick our asses if you get caught. Do not fuck up my wedding."

"Come on, Thad. Let his ass get beaten to death. We need to head back to the villa."

I ignored the comments from the guys and continued down the path.

As if sensing me coming toward her, Kai said something to the group and slipped from the middle of the circle of women dancing.

It took less than a minute for her to meet me at a remote part of the beach close enough to hear the music, but far enough to keep prying eyes from seeing us.

She stopped a few feet from me. Fucking hell, that body. I'd spent most of the night before balls-deep inside her, but she staggered me every time I saw her.

"You're trespassing on bride night. There are severe consequences if you get caught."

Instead of responding, I took the two steps to reach her, cupped the back of her head, and pulled her lips to mine.

"Jax." She gasped in surprise and then almost immediately slid her fingers into my hair, fisting it and meeting the demands of my mouth with hers.

"I have to have you." I glided my hands up her bare back, untying her bikini top. "You have to remember how crazy it makes me to watch you dance like that."

"We can't. Not here." Her fingers contradicted her words as they worked the buttons of my shirt. "This is insanity."

"Insanity is craving you every day for the last two years and only now being able to touch you."

I shrugged out of my shirt, letting it fall to the sand. Her nails raked my chest while her teeth nipped my neck. My cock jumped in reaction. She rarely was the actual aggressor when it came to us. Submitting to me was what got her off. She was always so controlled in her work that letting go in bed was a release for her.

Before I realized what she was doing, she dropped to her knees, gripping the buckle of my belt. She pulled the leather free, popped the button of my shorts, and managed to work the zipper down past my hard-as-fuck cock.

"Kai," I groaned as my cock sprang free, bobbing in front of her face.

She gripped the base and glanced up with a wicked gleam in her dark-brown eyes.

Her tongue poked out, rimming the straining head and dipping along the slit on the tip.

She hummed. "I love the way you taste. It's so earthy and raw. Until you, I never enjoyed giving head."

I narrowed my gaze. "The last thing I want is you thinking of going down on other men when my dick is an inch from your mouth."

The smirk on her lips told me she'd said that on purpose to rile me. She knew I hated hearing about her past lovers, few as they were. She always brought out the caveman in me. She was mine.

"Is this that you want?" She engulfed me in her wet, hot mouth.

"Fuck." My fingers fisted her hair, wanting so desperately to make her take me as deep as possible.

At that moment, she swallowed, contracting the back of her throat. My eyes nearly rolled into the back of my head from the pleasure.

This was a maddening torture. I couldn't get enough. Especially, the feel her lips wrapped around me. The heat of her wet mouth. The caress of her fingers pumping me with each movement.

Spurts of precum oozed from my cock, and I gritted my teeth, trying not to lose it like a teenage boy.

As if sensing my impending loss of control, she rubbed her tongue along the vein that ran down the underside of my dick and then took me as deep as she could possibly go and hummed, the vibration an evil torture.

"Kai. Stop or I'm going to come down your throat."

There was a war in her gaze. She loved sucking me off but she also knew the orgasm awaiting her.

Making her decision, she released me with a pop, her lips swollen and wet from her saliva and my precum.

Damn, this woman was sexier than any other on earth.

Did she have any idea what I'd do for her if only she'd ask? I was hers.

"I want to fuck you now. Sit." She pointed to my shirt.

I lifted a brow at her order.

Yeah, my dick was hanging out for anyone to see, but it turned me on to no end to see her eyes full of heat and demanding desire.

"Please, Jax. I want this memory of you here." The change of her words from command to plea wasn't something I expected.

I rubbed a thumb along her mouth before following her instructions.

It drove me insane that she still believed this was temporary. God, what would I need to do to prove to her I wanted forever?

Kai slid her hands into the thick layers of her skirt and shimmied out of her underwear. She took a step toward me, resting a hand on my shoulder, straddled my hips, letting her skirt flow around us, and then pushed her hot, soaking cunt down my engorged cock.

"Oh God," we both called out at the same time.

Nothing felt as good as her body wrapped around me. I only hoped I lasted. Her mouth had brought me to the point of coming, and I hadn't quite gotten my need under control. I'd be damned if she didn't come first.

I gripped her hips as her palms settled behind my neck. Slowly she rose and lowered, gyrating her hips in the exact way I'd imagined when I watched her dancing. It was twice as hypnotizing now with her staring directly into my eyes. Her gorgeous face flushed and her bare breasts tipped in hard points only a few inches from my face.

I had to taste those nipples. With one hand holding onto her back, I used the other to cup a perfect mound and sucked a hard pebble into my mouth.

"Jax." Kai's pace faltered for a second. "Yes, harder."

I feasted on her breasts, moving back and forth, giving her the slight bite of pain to bring her closer to her release.

"Please, I need," she moaned.

"I know what you need." Cupping her ass with both palms, I leaned back until I felt my shirt underneath me and proceeded to take over her movement.

I pumped up as my hands brought her down. It was hard and fast. Her nails dug into my shoulders, kneading the flesh as little cries of pleasure escaped her lips. My balls drew up, and I knew I wasn't going to last much longer.

I grabbed the thick tumble of hair at the back of her neck and tugged her forward, exposing her throat, and then bit down, not hard enough to break her skin but with the edge she needed to give her the pleasure-pain guaranteed to send her over.

She immediately responded. Her pussy quivered and then clamped down like a fist around my cock.

"Oh God. Y-y-y…es." Kai clenched her eyes tight, threw back her head, and lost herself, plummeting me into my own orgasm.

CHAPTER THIRTEEN

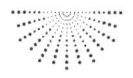

Kailani

"Time to wake up, sleepyhead."

I opened my eyes to see Jax leaning over me. It should have been a crime to look so good without trying.

I reached up and rubbed my finger along the stubble covering his jaw.

"You need to shave."

"It's on the agenda."

I yawned. "What time is it?"

"Four ten."

I groaned and turned my face into my pillow. "I had twenty more minutes to sleep."

"We need to talk before all the craziness of the wedding starts."

The seriousness of his tone had me moving to face him. The hard set of his jaw told me we were about to have the one conversation I'd hoped to avoid.

"I need to know if you want me to stay or not."

"Jax." I sat up. "It isn't that simple."

"Yes, it is. You either think we have a chance or you don't."

"And you believe we do?"

He scraped a hand through his sleep-messy hair. "I have no doubt we can make it work."

"Jax this isn't just about us. There are other factors."

"Like what?"

"The fact we come from different worlds. You're Hollywood and affluence. I'm a military brat."

"Who owns a huge percentage of this resort."

Shit, I'd forgotten he'd been part of the initial financing for the development of the property. Back then he'd offered to loan me more money to get a more substantial stake, but I'd refused, wanting to make the investment with my own savings.

"Jax, why can't you see I'll never fit into your world. I work for a living. I like working. You'd be better with a woman you could take to events and wouldn't give you as much trouble as I do. I know I'm not an easy person."

"And I am. Answer this, have I ever asked you to change, to fit into any mold?"

"No, you never told me to change, but you kept me as a separate part of your life. I won't ever be that again."

"Dammit, Kai, I told you why I did that. I wanted to keep you from the disaster my parents are. If I was ashamed of anyone or wanted someone to change, it would be my parents. They don't matter anyway. I haven't had a relationship with them since before you left me."

"Why didn't you tell me?"

"I didn't want to bring my shit home to you."

"And that's the problem. I'm the one person you're supposed to turn to, to stand beside you. Instead, you kept me far away from things."

"I can't change the past, Kai."

"I know. But I won't risk the same results again."

Hurt flashed on his face. "I really was fighting a losing battle. There was no chance for us from the beginning."

He slid from the bed, moving to the chair where his clothes lay. He put them on and then glared at me.

"You aren't blameless in this. You ran away. Instead of fighting for us, instead of confronting me, you got it in your head it was time to go and you moved on. You left. And I had to pick up the pieces. Did you know I'd left that weekend to get my grandmother's engagement ring from the family vault in Los Angeles? Did you know I was arranging for your family to fly in so I could propose to you? Or that Kevin had to be the one to see the aftermath of my shattered heart when I realized you ended us without looking back?"

What?

He wanted to marry me? I'd always hoped, but Jax rarely mentioned anything about a future with marriage. I'd thought he was happy with the way things were between us.

Had I read everything wrong?

My hands shook as I stared into his eyes and saw the truth of his words.

Why hadn't Kevin told me this?

"I didn't know." My throat burned.

"All I've ever wanted was what your parents have, what Thad's parents have." He grabbed his keys and moved to the stairs leading to the lower level of my bungalow. "It doesn't matter. It feels as if everything I've done to convince you of how much I love you was a complete waste of time. It only pushed you further away."

"It wasn't. It hasn't. I just need to process everything."

"Dammit, Kai. What more do I have to do to convince you I'm in this for good? I feel as if I'm fighting a losing battle." The resignation in his voice had panic churning in my stomach.

This couldn't be how it ended.

"Jax." I reached out. "Please don't go. Not like this."

At that moment, my alarm went off, making me cringe.

"You have wedding details to manage. I'll let you get to it."

Jax left, slamming the downstairs door.

―

"Wow, Mama, you're stunning," I said as I entered her bungalow and passed the hairdresser and makeup artist who'd helped her prep for the wedding.

I'd just left Lina in the capable hands of Raquel and her

team of people to make Lina's vision of wedding-day beauty a reality.

Now it was my turn to have my hair and makeup done. Hopefully they could hide the puffiness under my eyes.

My insides had felt shredded ever since Jax had left my place, and I'd barely managed to get the last-minute details organized. No, I actually hadn't. Raquel had noticed I wasn't entirely with it and had taken over.

"If you think I look good, then you need to see Kiana," my mother said. "She's truly gorgeous."

"She's an exact replica of you, so I wouldn't expect anything else."

Personality-wise, Kiana was completely Papa, but looks-wise, she was a younger version of Mama. Lina and I were a hodgepodge combination of our parents and grandparents.

Mama huffed. "All of my girls are beautiful."

"Yes, but I'm the prettiest." Kiana came out of a back room, wearing her strapless baby-pink gown.

It was simple with an empire waist that made her look almost delicate. I could definitely agree with her assessment of herself. In fact, she could have been the woman in front of the camera as much as the one behind it.

I wore the same style of dress, with a secret pocket sewn in to hide my phone since I was still in charge of the wedding.

Kiana stopped in front of me and frowned. "What's wrong? You look as if you've been crying."

"I'm fine."

"Umm, okay." She grabbed my arm, dragged me to a nearby couch, and pushed me down. "I call bull. Now spill it."

"Jax and I decided it would be better to end it." I closed my eyes for a brief second. "After the wedding, he's going to leave."

"What happened?" Mama asked, coming to sit by me and taking my hands in hers. "I could have sworn the two of you were next to go down the aisle."

"They're the only ones left, so of course they would have been next," Kiana interjected.

I ignored my sister and addressed my mom. "Mama, I can't put my heart on the line again."

"It's already on the line, baby."

My heart would heal—well, I hoped it would.

"Will you tell me now why you left in the first place? We've all wanted to know, but you never shared and we decided it was best to let you come to us with the information."

It was time to tell them. The abbreviated version.

"When Jax was present he was perfect, but when he wasn't, I was lonely and left feeling like a separate part of his life. He'd disappear at the drop of a hat to take care of things in LA, putting everything in our life on hold.

"He said it was to protect me from his parents. I just have a hard time accepting his explanation. I could have dealt with it if this was an occasional occurrence, but it had turned into a weekly thing. Vegas became a place he visited instead of where he lived.

"I know it was selfish but I wanted to be the most important person in his life. He was in mine." I hung my head, unable to look at my mom. "I'm ashamed to say leaving was easier than seeing if his love for me had died."

"Baby, that man never stopped loving you. It was always in his eyes." Mama tilted my chin up. "And this may be hard to hear, but you need to. If you love him, you have to accept whatever relationship he has with his parents."

"Why?" Kiana asked as she sat on the edge of the wooden coffee table in front of Mama and me. "They are such horrible people. I don't blame her one bit. Do you remember how they treated us like garbage? If it wasn't for Ani's intervention, I would have punched Jennine Burton in the face, paparazzi be damned."

Mama glared at Kiana, causing her to wince. She made a zipping motion to her lips.

If Kiana lasted more than three minutes without giving her opinion or making a remark, it would be a miracle.

"I'm going to tell you a story I haven't shared with any of you girls. When I met your father, neither of our parents were happy with us being together. In fact, Isaiah's mother thought I was a gold digger, since his family had generational money, much like Jax's father. And your Tutu Nima thought I was turning my back on our Hawaiian culture by marrying a man who knew nothing about our traditions and lifestyle and would move me away from my family."

This was seriously surprising news. "But Grandma and Tutu were such good friends. They acted as if they'd arranged your marriage from birth."

Tutu would say destiny had matched Mama and Papa. There had never been an ounce of dislike whenever Tutu would speak of Papa and especially not Grandma. They were thick as thieves and had traveled all over the world together as two widowed seniors.

Mama set a hand on my arm. "It took five years of marriage, five years of dislike, five years of horrible things said on both sides before things changed. In fact, it was your Papa nearly dying during a deployment to the Middle East for everything to change. I was pregnant with you, all alone at the base in San Diego, and scared out of my mind after hearing your Papa was airlifted to a hospital in Germany with a severe injury."

Mama pinched the bridge of her nose. "It still makes me want to cry remembering that time. I'd contacted both moms to let them know what was happening, expecting them to ignore my calls as they'd done since the day your Papa and I eloped. But they both answered and arrived on my doorstep within twenty-four hours.

"The resentment I'd had toward them disappeared the second they hugged me. And by the time your Papa returned home to us, both moms were friends and understood each other."

I sighed. "Mama, I'm not sure there's hope for that kind of reconciliation with Jax's parents. They aren't like Grandma or Tutu. They are about image and status. It isn't about what's best for Jax. The stories he told me about his childhood were filled with sacrificing Jax's happiness for advancing his parents' careers and lives."

"Then answer these questions, is Jax like them?"

I frowned. "Of course not. He's nothing like them."

"Then be honest with yourself—did he keep you from his parents because he was ashamed of you or because he wanted to protect you from them?"

I knew what she was trying to do. To show me I'd run for no reason, that I'd let my insecurities get the best of me.

My lips trembled. "Because he was protecting me."

"Would you rather he'd let you fend for yourself with his parents?"

"No. But I'd rather he had stood by my side when I dealt with them."

"Baby girl, men don't think the way we do. If they love someone—and I know Jax loves you—they want to slay your dragons and protect you from anything that could hurt you."

The image of Christopher and Jennine Burton as evil dragons made me want to smile. Then a wave of guilt hit me.

"Mama, I don't want to be the reason he has no relationship with his family, no matter how fucked-up they are."

I winced, realizing that I'd cussed.

Mama lifted a brow and said, "That isn't a decision you can make. It belongs to Jax. Your Papa made his own choices when it came to his parents. From where I'm sitting, Jax picked you."

I wanted it to be true; I wanted to have a life with him.

He was saying he would. Then why couldn't I accept it as real?

My vision clouded and a tear slipped down my cheek. "I'm scared that if he moves here, he'll regret it."

"Dammit, Kailani, sometimes I want to shake some sense into you," Kiana burst out. "Sorry, Mama, but you're being too gentle with her. The only way to get through to her is by being blunt. Are you worth the risk? Is he worth the risk? If the answer is no, then walk away. Stop going back and forth, make a fucking decision and stick to it. If you have regrets later, then it's on you. I swear, you can be such a dumbass."

"Kiana, language." Mama pointed a finger at her.

"No, Mama. I'm tired of this. The man is head over heels in love with this idiot, but he only has so much energy to spend on trying to convince her to take the chance. I'm of the mind to tell him to move on. He deserves someone who loves him with the same intensity he feels."

"I do love him. I love him so much that I couldn't imagine living a life where I was second to everything else in his life."

"But you weren't." Mama wiped the tears on my face with a tissue she'd pulled from a box on a side table. "Perception isn't always reality."

"I know." I hiccupped. "I shouldn't have left him the way I did. I should have confronted him with the way I was feeling, instead of shutting down. I should have—"

Kiana cut me off. "*Should have* doesn't belong in this

conversation. It's what you're going to do now that matters."

Kiana was right—I had to stop living in the past and letting my fears win out. I either took the risk or lived out the rest of my life as I had the last two years.

Alone.

Taking a deep breath, I whispered, "You're right."

"Of course, I am. Just because I'm younger than you doesn't mean I'm not wiser than you."

God, I loved this girl.

"Yes, yes, on this matter you are." I leaned over, kissed Mama on the cheek, and then smiled at Kiana.

"Now that we've figured out your love life, go have your face fixed. You look like hell." Kiana smirked and pointed at the room where the makeup artist waited.

CHAPTER FOURTEEN

JAX

My breath caught as Kai came out with Kiana and Ani. Kai was a vision. The simple, strapless pale-blue gown showed off her curves in all the right places and gave me visions of what it would be like if we were the ones getting married.

After this morning, I wasn't sure if it was only ever going to be a fantasy. I couldn't get through to her, and my parents were always going to be a problem for us.

I'd barely acknowledged the pair since they'd arrived on the island. I knew there was no hope of making them see their actions in my life had caused a rift that could only be mended if they met me halfway. No matter if Kailani and I were together or not, I couldn't let them manipulate my life anymore. Maybe I was a bad son, but at this point, I couldn't care less.

"Everyone, you know your positions. Time to pair up,"

Raquel announced as she looked at her watch. "The music will start in exactly three minutes."

I moved to where Kai stood. Her beautiful deep brown eyes lifted to mine.

"You're stunning."

She licked her lush lips. "Thank you. You look handsome too."

Without thinking, I leaned down to kiss her, and to my surprise, she lifted her face and the knot in my stomach eased. Maybe there was hope for us, after all.

"Oh no, you don't." Raquel set a hand on my chest and pushed me back. "You will not mess up her makeup. Her horoscope said she has a romantic moonlit night ahead. So, save the smooching for later. Right now, we have a timetable to follow."

Well, I guessed we couldn't argue with Raquel's daily horoscope predictions. I would take any positive prediction about our future that I could get, especially after this morning.

I stepped back and offered Kai my arm. We moved into position behind Thad.

Thad pulled at the collar of his white suit. It was surprising to see him nervous. He was always so composed and sure of himself.

I would have made some wisecrack about his anxiety if I wasn't in the same restless state.

Kai's fingers flexed against my jacket sleeve. "Jax?"

"Yes." I peered down at her.

She opened her mouth to say something, but Raquel

spoke instead. "Okay everyone, you know what to do. One minute and counting. Lina is in the wings waiting for everyone to take their places."

Thad glanced behind him and immediately turned around when he saw Raquel marching toward him.

"Don't even think about trying to get a peek. You can see Lina when she meets you at the altar."

"Yes ma'am." He turned around and then muttered, "That woman's a tyrant."

The music started and per Raquel's cue, we began our trek up from the hotel to the pastor waiting for us on the shores of the beach.

A quarter of the way up the long pathway, Kai said in a low voice while smiling to the wedding guests who were waiting for us, "Jax?"

"Yeah."

"I'm sorry."

"For what?"

"For doubting you, for doubting us."

This was a turnabout I hadn't expected. For her to apologize, something must have happened. I wanted to have hope but I refused to believe things had changed from this morning until she said it clearly. "What does that mean?"

"It means..." She took a deep breath. "I want us to work. I want to be with you."

"You want me to stay after everyone leaves?"

"Yes."

"Does that mean you're going to marry me?" I asked as

we approached the flower-covered aisle leading to the beachfront altar.

Her steps faltered for a split second. "Ask when it's time, when I can say yes, not today. Today is about Lina and Thad."

That meant she would say yes in the future. At least, I hoped. This pint-sized woman had me so twisted with wanting her in my life. Never had I chased a woman like this. Then again, I'd never loved a woman like this either.

"Just so we're clear. I wasn't going to leave even if you expected me to. I would have worn you down sooner or later."

"Of course, you weren't. You march to your own drummer."

She had me there.

When we reached the altar and were about to separate, she looked up at me, backdrop of the ocean giving her an ethereal aura.

"I love you, Jax," she whispered and then pulled free of my hold, knowing she'd floored me with her confession.

In fact, my heart felt as if it would explode. The only thing that would be better was if we were alone when she said those words.

I took my spot next to Thad as the rest of the wedding party got into position on their respective sides of the flower-covered wedding arch.

The wind picked up, carrying with it the scent of saltwater and flowers. At the same time, the clouds overhead shifted and beams of sunlight shined down on the altar.

This had to be a good sign, not just for Thad and Lina, but for Kai and me. Or if Raquel had anything to say about it, the horoscope she'd read to me this morning had come true. It had said something about the sun brightening my heavy heart and giving me clear direction.

I guess I owed Raquel an apology for rolling my eyes and tell her it was wishful thinking.

Now here I was, about to watch my best friend marry the woman of his dreams, while mine wanted to give us a real chance, a real future.

Damn, hearing three words from Kai's lips had turned me into a sap.

The wedding march started, and I heard Thad say, "Finally."

One day I'd get my "finally." One day Kai would say yes.

I watched Kai and the way her eyes lit up the second Lina came into view. A tear spilled down Kai's cheek.

I knew I should have been looking down the aisle at Lina but I couldn't move my attention from Kai. The pure joy on her face told me she wouldn't have gone so above and beyond to create this perfect wedding for her baby sister if she didn't have a hopeless romantic side.

As if sensing me staring at her, she looked my way. All her shields were down in a way I hadn't seen since our time in Vegas. She was finally letting me in.

"I love you too," I mouthed.

I shifted my attention to Lina as she reached the bottom of the altar. She winked at me, telling me she'd caught what I'd said to Kai.

Well fuck, I hadn't meant for that to happen.

Pretending nothing significant had passed between all of us, Lina kissed her parents and stepped toward Thad. I handed Thad a lei, custom-designed to match Lina's gown, and Kai gave one to Lina. The couple exchanged the leis, draping them over each other's heads.

At that moment, Kevin moved from his place by the groomsmen and lifted a conch shell. He blew into it four times, turning with each blow to invite the four elements of earth to bless the wedding.

Over the years, I'd learned how important the traditions of Hawaiian culture were to the Alexander family. Being in Bora Bora wasn't going to change this fact.

Even Isaiah, who'd grown up on the mainland, had immersed himself in his wife's traditions and raised his family with them as part of their everyday lives. For them, it wasn't something for tourists to play with as an added bonus to a destination wedding but about their heritage and family history.

The ceremony lasted for another thirty minutes, with a period of silence to remember those family members who had passed away, and then closing with the laying of the lava rock wrapped in a ti leaf on the ground and the traditional celebratory kiss.

Cheers shouted all around as the newly married couple made their way down the aisle and we followed.

Kai beamed with happiness and then whispered, "Once we make it through the reception, I can breathe. Want to help me celebrate later?"

"Absolutely. Does this mean I won't get to see you again for hours? You know we still need to have a long talk."

"Yes, I know. But it's time for me to finish off my maid-of-honor duties."

Kai slid her arm free of mine, but I caught her wrist.

"Jax, I have to go."

"Tell me again, Kai. I need to be sure I heard you correctly the first time."

Her lips curved at the corners, and she lifted up on tiptoes, brushing a kiss against my lips. "I love you."

And in the next second, she was gone, grabbing a phone from Raquel and marching down the hallway to the bridal dressing area.

I turned to make my way to where the groomsmen were gathering and came to an abrupt halt as my parents stood in front of me.

"Son, your mother and I would like a word with you."

I took a deep breath and braced myself for whatever lecture was about to come.

"Let's go somewhere more private," I said.

I wouldn't put it past my mother to cause a scene. She had a habit of living out her reputation as a diva to a tee.

From what my grandparents had told me, my mother hadn't always been so self-absorbed. There was a time when she'd been known as one of Hollywood's kindest souls. A person who'd give the shirt off her back to make someone else's life better.

It saddened me to know the ruthlessness she'd endured

as an actress in Hollywood had turned her into the cold, self-centered woman that I'd only ever known.

We moved over to the area where the wedding had taken place.

"Go ahead." I slid a hand into my pocket and waited.

"You should treat us with more respect," my mother started.

And with those words, the sentiment for the woman she used to be disappeared.

"I could say the feeling is mutual."

"I have no idea where we went wrong." She threw up her hands.

"Maybe it started when you'd have rather pawned me off on a nanny, Pops, or the Olivers. I spent more time with Thad's parents than you." I glanced back at Justine and Kristy Oliver. The couple's attention was on us instead of their family who'd flown in for their son's wedding.

"How dare you criticize us?" My mother's outrage was comical. "Say something, Christopher."

"Jennine, this isn't helping."

"I couldn't agree more," I added.

That resulted in a loud huff.

How the fuck I'd survived childhood with her was beyond me.

Oh, that's right, they hadn't raised me.

"Jackson, it's time you stopped this shipbuilding nonsense and take the reins of the company," my father said. "I'm getting old and I want you at the helm."

How many times was I going to have this conversation?

"I made my position clear the last time we spoke. I do not want Burton Productions, nor the strings that come with it."

"You'd turn your back on your inheritance. You'd let it pass to your cousin Richard?" My father seemed as baffled now as he'd been the last five times I'd had the same conversation with him.

Richard was a good man and deserved it. He'd worked for my father from the time he'd graduated from college. He also could manage my parents in a way I could never do.

"Yes. Richard loves the business and has doubled profits since he's taken the lead on the majority of projects."

"This is all because of that no-name tramp he's seeing again. I will not have it."

"Mother, I'd watch what you say when it comes to Kailani Alexander."

I would never understand why they even bothered to come to this wedding when they couldn't stand Kai or any of her family. No, that wasn't true. It was about saying they were part of something exclusive, something only those in the "in-crowd" were invited to.

What would my mother say if she knew the only reason Thad had invited them was out of courtesy to his parents and the long history our families shared. Everyone, including Justine and Kristy Oliver, knew what my parents thought of Kai, and as an extension any Alexander, including Lina.

"I'm only stating the truth. She isn't one of us, no matter if Thad has raised her status by marrying her sister."

If this was anything like what Kai had experienced, then I couldn't blame her for leaving, especially when I kept trying to fix every little issue my parents had.

"Talking to you is useless. You're never going to see that insulting the woman I plan to marry is an exact way to keep me from having any relationship with you."

I turned my back to them and started down the path to the main building.

I heard my mother shout, "If you choose her, don't ever come crawling back to us."

I ignored the words and looked at Thad and his parents, who waited for me. They were my family. And the one the Alexanders had adopted me into.

CHAPTER FIFTEEN

Kailani

"Thanks, Raquel. I swear you'll get a raise for putting up with my crazy family," I said into my phone as I made my way to the reception hall.

Thad and Lina were ready to make their grand entrance as husband and wife, and I was due at the head table to finish out my maid-of-honor duties.

I'd helped Lina change out of her gorgeous white ultra-feminine wedding gown with lots of flowing fabric and into something befitting the Hollywood starlet she was, a super sexy, form-fitting gown with an open back and sky-high heels.

"I won't say no to a raise, but I think you deserve one too."

"I'll be sure to pass on the evaluation to the Lykaioses."

"I already did."

I stopped midstep. "Please tell me you didn't actually do that."

"Is there static on the line?" Raquel *shh*ed with fake static. "I can't hear you, boss. I'll catch you later."

She hung up and I shook my head. I couldn't be sure whether she'd done as she said or was pulling my chain.

Slipping my phone back into my clutch, I made a quick stop in the restroom to make sure my makeup was still up to snuff and then walked toward the side entrance to the ballroom.

"I hope you're happy. You got what you wanted." The venom-filled words spoken behind me as I set my hand on the door handle had my back stiffening.

Fuck. Thirty more seconds and I'd have been home free.

I'd managed to avoid Jennine Burton since she'd arrived with her husband, and hoped to keep avoiding her. Now it looked as if my luck had run out.

I turned to face Jennine. She was beautiful, with barely a trace of her age on her skin, but nothing could change the ugly under the surface or the hatred in her eyes as she glared at me.

I guessed I'd have to get used to it, since Jax and I were planning a future together. It still made me cringe to think she'd be my children's grandmother one day.

Bracing myself for whatever was wrong in Jennine's world, I said, "Mrs. Burton, I have no idea what you are referring to."

"Don't act so coy. I lost my son because of you."

I will not take the bait. I will not take the bait.

With as much of a smile as I could fake, I said, "Let me repeat. I have no idea what you are referring to."

She cocked a hand on her hip. "I find it hard to believe you don't know that my son hasn't come home or had anything more than a surface relationship with us in the last two years. Because of you, he's turned his back on his legacy and his responsibilities to Burton Productions."

I stared at her, not understanding what she was saying. Jax had mentioned he had nothing to do with his parents but I hadn't thought past the statement.

It also meant she had no idea we were together again. Well, Jax and I still had to figure out the details.

"Until a little over three weeks ago, I hadn't seen or heard from Jax in years."

"You think I didn't see your exchange during the wedding. Hell, everyone saw it. He isn't the type of boy to say his feelings so publicly unless it was something long-term."

No, it was because we'd never gotten over each other. But that information wasn't going to help this situation.

"As you said, you have a surface relationship with him. How would you know the way he thinks?"

"God, he's such a man. Shake your big tits and ass in his face and you're leading him around by the dick again."

Her vulgar words had me speechless.

She continued, saving me from finding a response.

"I saw those pictures in the tabloids. They got clear shots of you and your classless family dancing."

Heat and anger rushed into my body, and I gritted my teeth.

Taking a step toward her, I said, "Let me make something clear. You can say what you want about me but never, and I mean *never*, put down my family."

Knowing a dramatic scene was what she wanted, I took a calming breath and continued, "You have this need to label anyone who isn't in your perceived social standing as lower class. I will not put up with it anymore. We don't have diamonds flowing out of our pockets or a household staff to cater to our every need, but we are good people who have worked our asses off for everything we have."

"How dare you? We work just as hard, probably harder." Jennine cocked a hand on her hip and waved a finger in my face.

It took all my strength not to swat it away and punch her.

How could countless documentaries and Hollywood legend stories get it so wrong? She was nothing like the American sweetheart they'd made her out to be, but then again she hadn't starred in a film since before Jax was born. And any recent role she'd taken encompassed small cameos playing off her former fame.

"God, what happened to you? Where is the woman once known for her kind heart and soul?"

Something flashed in her eyes that almost resembled pain, but disappeared just as fast.

"You have no idea what it takes to make it in Hollywood."

Hollywood was known for chewing up the innocent until there was barely anything left of the original person before spitting them out. It was hard to imagine Jennine Burton as one of them. But the woman before me wasn't the one whose movies my mother and aunts loved watching.

"You're right. I won't argue with that point, but it doesn't excuse your behavior now. You were a hard-working actress once upon a time, a good enough one to win an Oscar. But that was decades ago. Tell me what you've achieved recently. Besides alienating your son with all your antics."

She grabbed my arm. "Listen here, you little slut. I refuse to let you dig your claws into him again. You're nothing but a gold digger. That boy deserves better. Don't think you'll get a penny of our money."

I shook her hand free and rubbed where her nails had left crescent-shaped marks.

"You are seriously delusional. I don't need anything from Jax."

She laughed in that way one would expect the evil queen from a children's cartoon to do. She really had lost her acting edge.

"It's always about money."

This conversation was going nowhere. I tried to have compassion for her, for what she must have dealt with, but the second she touched me with anger, any sympathy I had for her disappeared.

"Look, I'm only going to say this one time. I make plenty of money. In fact, I'm a partner in this resort." The surprise on her face made me want to smirk, but I refused to stoop to her level. "I don't need a penny from Jax. Why would I, when I live in paradise with a house on the beach?"

I turned toward the doors. I had to get away from this self-centered woman. I'd mastered handling difficult guests, so why was I letting her get to me?

Because it hurt to know people who were supposed to be family behaved this way.

I had to accept I'd never have the loving relationship Thad's parents had with Lina or what my parents had with Cora and Ani.

Once Lina and Thad made their entrance, I was going to down some shots of tequila.

"Don't think this is over."

I should have kept walking but I was done with this.

I faced her again. "Why are you so fixated on me? This is a conversation you need to have with Jax."

"My relationship with my son is none of your business."

"That's right, it's not. Keep me out of it. Jax and I are trying to see where this goes. You can try all you want but it won't scare me off."

She smiled and lifted a brow as if she'd won. "It did before."

There was no point in denying it when she was partly

right. "It won't again. I've learned from my mistakes. You seem to want me to make them over and over again." I sighed.

"Do you really think he'll marry you?"

"Yes, he will." We both froze as Jax stepped from around the corner. "There's no doubt about it."

CHAPTER SIXTEEN

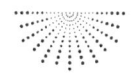

JAX

"Jax." My mother moved in my direction, but I sidestepped her, going toward Kai.

When I'd heard the words my mother was spewing at Kai, I wanted to step in and protect her from the venom. Then I realized Kai was holding her own.

I'd intervened when we were officially behind on the schedule Kai had set.

I stopped a foot from Kai, setting a hand on her waist before leaning down to kiss her forehead. "Raquel sent me out here to find you. Are you ready?"

"Yes."

I offered her my hand and she took it.

"I guess I'm on Raquel's bad side."

"Possibly."

I walked her to the side door.

"We are not done here," my mother said.

"Yes, Mother, we are. Safe travels."

We entered the ballroom to cheers, as if we were the newlyweds.

"God, how late was I?"

"Five minutes, tops."

Kiana tapped an imaginary watch on her wrist, making Kai blush.

She really was adorable when she was embarrassed.

"She's never going to let me live it down."

I helped Kai into her seat next to where Lina would sit.

"Save a dance for me." I trailed my fingers over the back of her neck and felt her skin prickle with goose bumps.

"Definitely."

The next two hours were filled with cheers, speeches, tears of happiness, and dinner.

When I finally got a chance to dance with Kai, all I wanted to do was find a quiet spot alone with her.

"Care to dance?" I asked Kai.

She looked over to the crowded dance floor. "Not really." She threaded her fingers with mine. "I have a better idea. Are you up for an adventure?"

"Sure."

"Let's go out the side so no one follows us. The last thing I want is anyone to find my favorite spot on the island."

"This sounds interesting."

She led me out of the ballroom, through the resort kitchens, and out to the service exit where a golf cart sat.

We climbed in and drove down a dark pathway that had

me wondering how Kai could see anything. We remained silent until we reached a gate where she typed in a code and then placed her hand on a reader.

"This place must be exclusive for all this security."

She smiled. "Very exclusive."

After the gate opened, we followed a pathway illuminated by what I could only describe as looking like lightning bugs.

The Lykaioses had gone a bit crazy with the hidden tech on this patch of the island.

We parked in a sandy area near the far end of the beach closest to her bungalow and farthest away from the main resort.

"Come." Kai jumped out of the golf cart. "No wait, first strip."

"What?"

"You heard me. Get naked." She kicked off her heels, throwing them on the seat and then reached behind her to unzip her dress.

"What about cameras? No one gets to see you naked but me."

She rolled her eyes. "Okay, caveman. No need to worry about anyone seeing my lady bits. I disabled the cameras when I punched in the code."

She dropped her bridesmaid dress, letting it pool at her feet and exposing her naked breasts and tiny thong.

Fuck, she was breathtaking under the glow of the moonlight.

She picked up her gown and dropped it on the side of the cart.

"You're still dressed." She shimmied out of her underwear and placed it atop her dress.

"Are we going skinny-dipping?"

She gave me a wicked grin that made my cock jump. "Possibly."

Swimming naked with Kai had been a fantasy of mine for as long as I could remember.

"Not sure if that's such a good idea. The paparazzi have been circling the resort ever since news broke about all the high-profile celebrities arriving on the island."

The idea of any of those fuckers getting a shot of her and the anger it caused helped me understand why people punched nosy papz in the face.

"This is private property with its own security. About three hundred feet from shore, there's a sensor system disguised as buoys marking shallow water. If anyone crossed over them, a series of low-voltage lights will alert us."

"How the hell do you know this?"

"Because this is my land. I bought it as part of my offer to move here. Kevin installed the security since he had to make sure his sister was protected."

I stared at her. "So, am I understanding you correctly? You own the property we're on and the bungalow you live in."

"Yes. Does it make a difference that I only want you for your hot body and not your money?"

I glared at her. "I've never thought that."

She walked over to my side of the golf cart and set her hand on my chest.

"I was kidding." She lifted up and brushed a kiss on my jaw. "Bad joke."

She slipped away before I could grab her.

"Are you going to get naked or not? You'll want dry clothes to change back into."

I quickly shucked my shoes and suit. I moved toward her.

Her gaze landed on my hard cock. She licked her lips, making me hold in a groan imagining her mouth wrapped around my cock.

"Swim now. Give me a blowjob later."

"Grab the towels from the bag on the back seat and follow me."

We took a surprisingly clear path down, dimly lit by strategically placed lights to a small cove with rocks all around.

Kai walked to the edge and looked over her shoulder. "Drop the towels and meet me on the other side."

Before I could say anything, she dived in, disappearing for a few seconds and then popping up about fifty feet out and climbing out on the other side of the cove.

She squeezed the water from her hair and waved me over. "Jax, come on."

I moved to the edge, setting the towels on a boulder, and jumped in. The water was clear, barely even a trace of salt, clean enough to drink. That was when I realized this was a natural freshwater pool, fed by the streams and rain on the island. It was separated from the ocean by the thin strip of land and rocks where Kai was standing now.

I'd heard about these freshwater pockets but most were on private land and inaccessible to the public. I could understand why. This was a private oasis I wouldn't want to share.

I swam toward Kai and pulled myself up onto the ledge. Shaking the water from my face, I saw the silhouette of my yacht anchored in the distance and the reflection of light from the house I'd built for Kai on the ocean water.

How would she react when she learned I'd been near her from the time she'd moved to Bora Bora?

"Sit. It's time we talked." She pointed to a smooth rock, snapping my attention back to her.

I sat, and she immediately straddled me, the lips of her pussy dangerously close to my cock. The water may have cooled my arousal but having her heat pressed against me was too tempting.

"I'm not sure this is such a good idea. All coherent thoughts are moving south, and sex on a rocky ledge is probably not as comfortable as it may seem in our heads." I tried to lift her off by the waist but she tightened her thighs around mine.

"I'm sure you have enough willpower to resist." She laughed and wrapped her arms around my neck.

"Then I suggest you stop wiggling on my dick."

"Jax?" The amusement in her tone evaporated and grew serious, bringing my focus fully on her face.

"Yes, baby."

"Are you sure you'll be happy living here?"

I stared into her eyes. The uncertainty there made me want to shake her.

Cupping the back of her head, I drew her face to mine. "Absolutely certain."

It was time to tell her how certain I was.

"I have a confession." I ran a thumb over her lower lip. "Hopefully you won't punch me in the gut for it."

I glanced toward my ship, the *Kailani*.

"You mean about the fact you're the reclusive billionaire who lives on his mega-yacht off the coast of this island? Or that you're the man who's building the house made of glass on the cliff over there?" She pointed toward the house.

I swallowed. Fuck, I was in trouble.

"How did you know?"

"I didn't until you glanced in the direction of the ship and then the house. Only someone who knew the lay of the island and what was on it could spot things from here, especially with how dark it is."

This had the potential to go very badly.

"Then I guess you know I've been here for a while now."

She nodded and then rested her forehead against mine.

"Why did you wait so long?"

"Because I wasn't sure if you'd welcome me or try to shoot me."

She lifted her head. "I'm serious."

"So am I. Losing you destroyed me inside. I was scared

to make the same mistakes again, and if I didn't know what I'd done, I couldn't avoid them."

She sighed. "I shouldn't have left. I let my impulsive side dictate my decisions. So instead of confronting you about what was going on in our relationship, I ran. I hurt you. I hurt me. I'm sorry, Jax."

"I'm sorry too."

Tears glistened in her eyes.

"Don't cry, love. We're getting a second chance to get it right."

"I promise not to run ever again."

I smiled and drew her slowly to me for a light kiss. "Good. Then it will keep me from moving across the world again."

A giggle escaped from her lips. "I can't believe you up and moved from Sin City to the middle of the Pacific for me. I must really have you pussy-whipped."

"Your pussy, as you put it, is a favorite place of mine, but it's this." I touched a finger over her forehead and then her heart. "And this, that holds me so tight. There's no way for a man to get over you, Kailani Alexander."

"I don't want you to get over me. I'm pretty stuck on you too."

"Then it's settled. You're marrying me and moving into that house I'm still trying to finish."

She shook her head. "Didn't I say to ask me when I can say yes?"

"I changed my mind. I'm not asking. It's a given.

Though marriage will come way before that house is ever done."

She laughed. "Everything works on island time here. Plus, getting supplies to the middle of the Pacific takes a while."

"Now I have one question for you." I stood, lifting her up with me.

She gripped my shoulders. "What?"

"Do I fuck you when we get back to shore or in your bungalow?"

She dropped her legs from around my waist and slid down my still-aroused body.

"How about both?" she said before diving in and then popping out of the water halfway between where I stood and the opposite shore.

I smiled at the gorgeous, mercurial woman who held my heart and knew life would never be dull with her, even in paradise. But it had been worth every minute of getting here.

The End

SNEAK PEEK

WRITTEN IN THE STARS - BOOK 6

Continue Reading for a Sneak Peek.

NORA

"You're really moving back?" I ask, unable to help myself. The sun is still high in the sky, and I raise my hand to shield it from blinding me as the opposing team snaps the football. The stadium is buzzing with anticipation for the opening game of the season, but I'm still in shock from my brother's revelation.

My brother, Owen, rolls his eyes. "I mean…why not? My football career died as soon as I blew out my knee. I stayed here to finish my degree then got sucked into a few opportunities but…."

My nephew, and Owen's son, Grady, pumps his fist into the air as the Red Hawks fumble the ball. He's completely oblivious to the adult conversation we're spouting, but he wouldn't understand the weight of it even if he were listening. There's just too much history for a little kid to comprehend, and I have to give Owen props for shielding him from it.

Owen joins in with his son's whooping and hollering, although I'm not sure if it's for Grady's credit or if it's because he wants me to drop the subject.

Yeah. Not happening.

When the crowd calms down long enough for me to hear myself think, I press, "But what?"

"Drop it, Nora."

"Nope. No deal. You could move anywhere with Grady now that his mom is out of the picture. I want to know why you want to move back to New Hampshire? Does it have something to do with an old flame you ditched before going off to college by chance?"

"Will you give it a rest?" he mutters under his breath.

"No. I won't. For women everywhere, I refuse to let you hurt her again. It was bad enough witnessing it the first time. Can you imagine how awful she felt? I mean––"

"Seriously, Nora. Will you please stop?" It's the desperation in his eyes that gets me to snap my mouth shut. He feels just as shitty about the circumstances as Saylor, his ex, did when he broke up with her. I just wish I could understand why he did it in the first place, and why he would feel the need to face her again after all these years. I mean, he has a kid for Pete's sake. Still, the pain is rolling off him in waves at the memory of everything he let slip through his fingers, so I bite my tongue.

Fed up with me staring at him, Owen grabs his son's hand and tugs him out of the bleachers as the crowd cheers at the completion of a twenty-yard pass across the field.

Remembering his manners, Owen asks, "We're going to get a hot dog or something. You want anything, Mama Two?"

"No, thanks. See you in a few."

He disappears up the steps with his son in tow. He'll be back. Then I'll apologize for being overly protective of his ex and her feelings. After that, he'll say it's okay, and we'll move on with life. But that doesn't mean I won't want a detailed update when he runs into her. And he will run into her.

What the hell is he thinking?

Lost in the comforting chaos surrounding me, I relax into my chair and watch the ball snap to our quarterback. I grew up in seats like this, cheering my brother on as he ran his way to the end zone over and over again. I still crave nachos and football jerseys every fall season and am grateful my brother was able to score us tickets to the first game of this season.

If only I hadn't scared him out of his seats with my meddling.

"Excuse me," a deep voice rumbles from the aisle. There's a soft slur to his voice that piques my curiosity. Looking up, I'm met with the richest brown eyes I've ever seen, even if they're a little glazed over from the caramel colored beverage in his hand. Just a hunch, but I don't think it's his first.

"Sorry, pre-gaming went a little longer than anticipated, but if I'd known I'd get to sit by a pretty little thing like you, I'd have cut it short," he adds with a teasing grin. Normally, the comment would roll right off me, but it's combined with that sexy smirk and an over-the-top wink that makes my insides tighten. I can't help but laugh before standing up in my seat to let him scoot past me. A few more muscular bodies follow him, each just as bombed as the last while also equally attractive. They look older than the usual frat boys, so I'm going to assume they're fans of the game or are alumni coming to root for their team. Just like my brother and me.

Brown Eyes surprises me by stopping on my right,

making his friends inch past him to get to their seats instead of him taking one further down.

Interesting.

Casually, I look up the stairs to see if my brother is coming back yet, but it's empty. Once the final guy scoots past me, I sit back down and try to act normal. Try, being the key word. I feel like I'm about to break into a sweat just because a cute guy happened to sit next to me at a football game. I sit up a little straighter.

Don't you dare look at him, Nora.

Don't.

Even.

Think.

About.

It.

Cheeks blazing, I peek over at him. He's looking at me with a full-blown grin plastered across his handsome face. Chiseled jaw. Straight, white teeth. Smoldering smirk that could melt the pants off a nun. It's a heady concoction.

I snap my attention back to the field. When I realize I'm holding my breath, my mouth forms a tiny 'o' shape before I let out the pent-up oxygen in my lungs. I take another peek. Yup. He's still looking at me. Still grinning. Still looking devilishly handsome.

And still driving me insane with his attention pointed directly at me instead of the game.

With a huff, I tuck my hair behind my ear and glance his way another time, only breaking eye contact when his cocky smirk almost makes me forget what I was going to say in the first place. "Is, uh…." Another peek. "Is there a problem?" I ask.

"No problem," he returns before tipping back his clear plastic cup and gulping down a bit more beer.

"Are you uh…you sure about that?" He's still staring at me with the whole cat-who-ate-the-canary look.

"Positive."

"Then why aren't you watching the game?"

"Because you're much more interesting to look at," he quips. "Can I ask you something?"

I can't help the awkward laugh that bubbles out of me before I mutter, "Sure. Ask away."

"Will you marry me?"

Covering my face in my hands, I laugh. Hard and uncontrollably.

"What's so funny?" he asks with faux outrage, though he's clearly enjoying my insane reaction to his equally insane proposition.

I laugh even harder, my cheeks so hot with embarrassment that I'm surprised I haven't burned up on the spot.

"Sorry, Gage." His friend pats him on the back, sloshing a bit of his drink onto the ground. "I'm pretty sure that's what you'd call rejection."

"Ah, come on, pretty girl. You can't reject me in front of my friends. They'd never let me live it down." With those same puppy dog brown eyes, he pouts for good measure.

"And what would you suggest I do?"

"Saying yes would be a good start," he teases before resting his elbow on the chair arm that separates us.

"You're charming when you're drunk; I'll give you that," I reply. There's a pinch in my cheeks from smiling so hard, but I can't help myself.

"Charming, huh? I can work with that." He tosses another wink my way before pointing out, "That wasn't a no, by the way."

I cover my mouth to prevent any more laughter from bubbling up, but it doesn't stop the pinch in my cheeks from amplifying.

"Come on," his friend interjects, leaning forward so that he can see me more clearly. "Throw the guy a bone. Say yes, will ya?"

"I believe this is called peer pressure at its finest."

"You wanna see peer pressure?" the stranger--Gabe?--asks with a mischievous grin. There's a time out on the field, so the crowd is relatively quiet, and our little interaction has slowly attracted the attention from strangers surrounding us. I can tell he's thriving on the attention while I feel like I'm having heart palpitations from it.

When he stands to his full height, towering over me, I realize what he's about to do.

No, no, no, no!

Reaching for his muscular forearm, I try to tug him back down, but it's like trying to pull a statue down that's been bolted to the ground. Useless.

"Don't you dare," I whisper-shout, not opposed to begging if it'll keep him from doing what I think he's about to do.

Throwing his head back, he laughs, and the sound goes

straight to my lower stomach. "Do you hear that?" he yells, demanding everyone's attention. "This pretty girl doesn't want me to propose in front of all of you on this beautiful day. You see, she isn't usually one for being the center of attention, but she's just too damn gorgeous to sit on the sidelines as she makes me the luckiest man in the world. Isn't that right, pretty girl?"

I scowl up at him, though I know he can see my curiosity and barely-restrained amusement no matter how hard I try to bury it.

The combination only encourages him to proceed.

There's no way he'd actually fake propose to me in front of all these people.

As if he can read my mind, he slowly lowers down to one knee before sliding my left hand into his.

"Will you, the most beautiful woman I've ever laid eyes on, the woman who captured my heart the moment we met…."--I snort before realizing the giant screen on the scoreboard is flashing with a live feed of his little speech--"Will you marry me?"

The entire stadium is silent, holding its collective breath the same way I'm holding mine. I can feel everyone's eyes on me. Hell, I can see it from the damn jumbotron.

"Come on, pretty girl," he murmurs in a low voice that's only meant for me. "Say yes. If you do, each and every fan in this place will have a good story to tell their friends when they get home, instead of a sob story about how you broke my heart."

Sneaky bastard. He's right, though. This would make a pretty epic story, which is the only reason why I nod my head up and down. The crowd goes wild. Whistling. Hooting. Screaming at the top of their lungs. The combination only seems to incite my fiancé further, encouraging him to stand up and tug me into his arms. Then he's kissing me.

I'm in shock for a solid two Mississippis before my body takes over. Fingers weaving into his soft, brown hair, heart racing a million beats a minute, I open my mouth and give a tiny piece of myself to an absolute stranger while knowing that I'll never be able to steal it back. When the taste of wheat explodes across my tongue, I grin against him.

"What's so funny?" he murmurs, keeping his arms around my waist

"Just thinking about how I was one hundred percent right in my initial assumption."

"And what's that?"

"You're charming when you're drunk."

"You should see me when I'm sober," he teases before dropping another quick kiss to my mouth. "Can I have your number?"

"You mean, so we can finalize our wedding arrangements?"

He laughs. "Something like that." His grip disappears as he searches his pockets. With pinched brows, he mutters, "Shit."

"What's wrong?"

"I left my phone in my car. I'll be back in a few."

I watch his sexy butt as he jogs up the concrete stairs before he disappears through the tunnel only to be replaced by a fuming Owen.

Cringing, I curl into my seat then wait for him and Grady to reach me.

"What the hell was that?" Owen demands, hooking his thumb over his shoulder.

My face reddens. "Nothing."

"You sure? 'Cause I'm pretty sure I just witnessed you getting proposed to on the screen."

"Yeah, what's up with that Mama Two?" Grady probes with his gangly little arms crossed over his chest, mirroring his father's posture. I shake my head and pull him into the seat beside me to prevent Owen from interrogating me any further. "It was nothing. Let's just finish the game."

I glance back at the tunnel, hoping to see my fake fiancé striding back to me with his confident swagger. But he never does. In fact, the only thing I'm gifted with are glares from his friends before they disappear from the stadium a few minutes later too.

What the hell was that?

Get the book here -> <u>Drowning In Love</u>

WRITING IN THE STARS BOOKS

Reluctant in Love by Rebecca Gallo (Book 1)
Bittersweet Love by Q.B. Tyler (Book 2)
Daring to Love by Karen Ferry (Book 3)
Price of Love by Erica Marselas (Book 4)
Intrigued by Love by Sienna Snow (Book 5)
Drowning in Love by Kelsie Rae (Book 6)
Fearless to Love by Harlow Lane (Book 7)
Jaded by Love by AJ Alexander (Book 8)
Measure of Love by C.M. Seabrook (Book 9)
Consumed by Love by CM Albert (Book 10)
Wandering in Love by Andi Jaxon (Book 11)
Crashing into Love by Hollis Wynn (Book 12)

BOOKS BY SIENNA SNOW

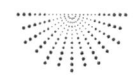

Rules of Engagement

Rule Breaker
Rule Master
Rule Changer

Politics of Love

Celebrity
Senator
Commander

Gods of Vegas

Master of Sin
Master of Games
Master of Revenge
Master of Secrets
Master of Control

Collections

Take Me To Bed
Reckless Rome (A Cocky Hero Club Novel)
Intrigued By Love

Street Kings

Dangerous King (Fall 2020)
Vicious Prince (Winter 2020)
Deceptive Knight (Spring 2020)
Ruthless Heir (Spring 2020)

Made in the USA
Monee, IL
30 January 2023